Hanging Ferns

A novel by S. D. Britt

PROFESSIONAL PUBLISHING MEETS POWERFUL PROMOTION

A wholly owned subsidiary of **TBN**

Dedication

To the one my heart loves the most and has loved me through the toughest of moments, never leaving, R. W., my soulmate.

My constant encourager, the one whose ears I've filled with countless words and never failing to answer when I call, my mother, you are exemplary; don't doubt it—believe it.

The voice of reason and the voice in my head, the most God-fearing man I know, my father, I am blessed to be your daughter.

Kristy, my most ardent supporter to finish this, thank you.

Michelle, you are of countless worth to me. When the world walked away, you stood with your arms open and held me. You whispered God's goodness and reminded me who I am in Him.

Ruth Ann, my bonus mom, you've always called me yours, and your friendship is precious to me.

1

"Charged, not convicted," the officer keeps telling me as he fingerprints my shaking hands. What little solace he tries to offer can't stop the flow of tears flooding my shirt. He and I both know these charges won't stick, but *I'm* still being arrested. It's a charge neither of us has ever heard. The worst fear settles in my mind: I will be locked in jail with actual criminals, and panic overwhelms me. How did this happen? This got out of control so quickly.

Three days ago, everything turned upside down. I was at my dad's eating pizza and popcorn—a delicacy considered our sacred family tradition—when someone banged on the wooden front door. The sound reverberated into my bones, shocking my system. I knew immediately who it was and why they were there. We all knew this could happen when the arrest warrants were issued, but it had been months, and settlements were already agreed on. I never thought this would really happen, and part of me believed it never would.

"It's probably your brother," my dad said as he walked toward the door, but I could hear the uncertainty in his voice. Even he didn't believe what he was saying.

I ran to the guest bedroom and peeked out the window

that looks out onto the street. I nearly collapsed at what I saw: four police cars and a K-9 unit. My body hit the ground immediately, and I began to pray for protection, guidance, and mercy because there was no getting out. I knew I had to do this no matter how badly my whole being resisted it.

My dad made his way into the darkened guest bedroom where I was. I'm not proud of how I handled myself at that moment or the state my dad saw me in, on the floor in the fetal position and having a full-blown panic attack.

"Audrey?"

"Yes, sir?" My voice shaking, knowing what he's about to tell me, but wishing he'll say something else, like "we've worked it out, and they've decided not to take you today." Of course, that's not what happened.

"Hey baby, you're gonna have to go with them."

"I know," I could barely get out through sobs wracking my body.

He whispered in my ear as he wrapped his arm around me and placed his hand on my chest, "They're going to handcuff you."

Dread began to rise as I ran to the bathroom to throw up. I sat on the cold bathroom floor, hugging the toilet and trying to grasp what was about to happen. I grabbed my phone and sent my mom a quick text: "I just got picked up.

My dad is working on bailing me out. Please pray for me."
Bad things don't happen to ignorant people, right? How
naïve I was. Mustering every ounce of bravery and courage,
I opened the front door and faced this impossible reality.

"Ma'am, please put your hands against the house and
spread your feet," the police officer with the glasses and
kind eyes said.

"You got anything in your pockets?" he added.

"No sir," I meekly replied.

The humiliation began right then on my dad's front
porch, in the ritziest gated neighborhood in town, searched
by the city police. Neighbors began to emerge from their
homes; nothing like this ever happened in their neighborhood.

I tried to be obedient but not weak. Three officers
looked on as he searched me. Not that I know much about
crime and police, but I didn't want to give the wrong impression that I'd do anything to get out of this, all while
trying to be compliant and do what I'm told—a fine line to
walk. I've heard horror stories about police and the power
they enjoy wielding. Being a young woman with no ability
to fight back made me an easy target.

As I sat in the back of the police car, I willed them to
hurry and leave, but the police officer was scanning the information on his computer in no apparent hurry at all. An-

other day on the job, he's young, short, and scrawny with a temper with every other sentence involving a four-letter expletive. I would be lying if I said his behavior and temperament didn't make me nervous.

"It says you have to go to Jefferson Parish, St. Charles Parish, then St. Tammany Parish. Jefferson won't pick you up until the morning. You'll stay the night in New Orleans City Jail," he quickly rattled off.

My head began to spin as I tried to wrap my brain around what he said. *Three* jails? Another client filed charges against me. The worst happened, and they've talked and no doubt encouraged each other to strengthen their case. They believe the worst about me. I wish they'd given me the opportunity to tell them what happened. My mind flashed back to reality as the puzzle pieces began to lock into place. It was Friday night before Christmas, which means everything had shut down. I would be stuck in jail for who knows how long because of the weekend and holidays. At that moment, I couldn't even cry where months before I couldn't stop. My body kicked into survival mode, and I did what I do best by asking questions and gathering information to figure out my angle.

"So, I have to stay the night in New Orleans City Jail tonight? Then go to Jefferson and bond out, then be picked up by St. Charles and bond out there too. And again with St. Tammany Parish?" I asked.

"Yep. Jefferson's real good about transporting people though, they should come to pick you up as soon as tomorrow morning. You do have to work around the holidays; Tuesday is Christmas Eve."

"Gosh," I sighed.

Finally, he sped out of the neighborhood and almost hit a car as he carelessly pulled onto the interstate. In the caged backseat, I slid the whole way on the plastic bench with my buckle loosely fastened. If we crashed, I'd be the first to go. At this point, my hands were still cuffed behind my back, and they began to hurt as metal pushed into my wrists. If this was a glimpse into how my time was going to go, I was more than apprehensive.

The ride only took twenty minutes, but to me, it felt like eternity, my mind racing as fast as the car. What was waiting for me? The only jails I've ever seen are on TV, and the thought makes me shudder; this isn't a made-for-TV script.

My first view of the jail is blurred by bright lights. As we get closer, I see that it's one story with peach-colored concrete, barbed wire-lined fences, and green metal roofing. We made our way into a breezeway, a sally port I later learned, with tall, chain link gates that enclosed either side of a garage. Every opening is closed, another stark reminder of where I'm headed, away from freedom and everything I hold dear. The driver opened my door, unbuckled me, and I slid out, my wrists finally relieved of the pressure.

"Stand here and don't talk," the young police officer commanded while he stood across from me.

I leaned against the padded wall as a female police officer with a sour face and too-tight ponytail walked my way. *This is it*, I mentally tell myself, *brace for what's coming*.

"Turn around," she sternly said as she unlocked my handcuffs. "Put your hands on the wall."

I did as she said, and she began to search me. She struggled with my back pocket buttons.

"I've never unbuttoned them," I nervously laughed, not sure how to act.

She gave up and replied, "Keep your hands behind your back and follow this red line to the set of footprints over there." She pointed to a yellow set of footprints around the corner against the wall. The thought doesn't escape me that ordinarily, I'd think the footprints were juvenile and would probably get a good laugh. Not now.

I did as I was told and faced another young woman with a curly wig, hot pink lipstick, too much perfume, and fake eyelashes behind a raised desk. She rapid-fire asked me questions like, "Do you have a history of seizures? Have you ever been to jail before? Diagnosed with an STD? Any chance you're pregnant? Do you have a family history of diabetes or heart issues?" She asked them so fast I attempted to keep up and not have her ask them twice. My mantra instantly became, *be invisible and not an inconvenience.*

"Walk down there," she nearly yelled, pointing to the next officer waiting on me. No one looks me in the eye or even looks at me at all. I'm the sole product on this assembly line. I walked the long red line, looking into the empty cells and wondering how I got here. Shock overcame my mind and body that I couldn't think clearly, and my knees were shaking uncontrollably.

A man, another officer younger than me with gold-rimmed '80s style glasses, attempted small talk with me, but afraid to give him the wrong impression, I didn't respond. Could I trust him? He began his barrage of questions.

"What's your weight?" he asked.

"125," I responded quickly.

He stared at me for what felt like an eternity. I couldn't tell whether he was joking or trying to be mean. I shrugged and repeated, "One hundred twenty-five." Not the time I want to joke about my weight. Thankfully he went back to typing on his computer and continued the process of what I now know as booking me in. I'll become acquainted with this process over the next week.

"Charged, not convicted," he says as he finishes fingerprinting my right hand. I now realize he's kind and obviously sees how terrified I am.

"Look right here," he says, pointing to a camera.

Here we go. My mugshot that hopefully won't be plastered all over the news. Guilty until proven innocent, the opposite of what I've always been told. I stare at the camera, willing it to display my story. My side. Let this picture be my voice while I'm here. Let one single picture tell who looks on that there is more to this headline. From now on, I will never look at a mugshot the same and assume guilt when the headline reads, "Charged."

All the officers are talking amongst themselves, and I barely hear one of them say, "Jefferson won't pick her up until Monday." I nearly collapse. I want to scream. Two nights in this place? I internally tell myself to pull it together. There is no getting out of this, no matter how much I will it to go away. Orleans Parish is holding me for Jefferson Parish; there's no bond for me to get out. I'm trapped in this jail for three days.

The woman who initially searched me tells me to follow her. We walk to an enclosed wardrobe room filled with plastic canvas bags that line the walls. Each bag has a mugshot attached indicating whose belongings are inside. Sad, hollow faces displayed in grainy black and white pictures stare back at me.

"How tall are you?" she asks from behind a desk, shaking me from my thoughts.

"5'4"," I reply.

She disappears to the back of the room. She's carrying an orange jumpsuit as she heads back to me. This can't be real. I stand in a corner that resembles a shower, surrounded by cement walls and floors. The smell of body odor and feet fills my nose. She hands me the jumpsuit and my own plastic canvas bag with my mugshot. The first time I glimpse the picture, I don't recognize myself. Enlarged pupils and fear written all over my face. My mind is at war. Over an hour ago, I was sitting by the fire in my dad's living room surrounded by family. Cold, hard edges and isolated strangers replace any kind of comfort I just left. Sorrow permeates every part of my soul. I want to sit and cry and feel sorry for myself.

"Get undressed and put your clothes in this bag."

The humiliations continue when I undress in front of her. She tells me I can keep my bra and underwear, a small victory, the one thing that is truly mine. Not knowing when I'll be able to wear my clothes again, I fold them, say a silent goodbye, and quickly dress into the ensemble she's given me, complete with a T-shirt, jumpsuit, socks, and rubber slippers—all orange. I've never hated a color more than I do now. Shame overcomes me when I fasten the final button of the oversized jumpsuit. This isn't real. I half-expect to wake up from this horrific nightmare, but no amount of pinching will wake me from this reality.

When I'm done dressing, she motions for me to come to her.

"Give me your wrist."

I hesitantly put my wrist out, and she places a hospital band-like bracelet on me that reads, "Tribb, A. 76059."

"You need to make a phone call?"

My heart leaps, "Yes, ma'am."

I'm placed in the first cell I've ever entered. A clogged metal toilet sits in the corner, and I nearly gag. An old pay phone hangs on the wall by the door, and I pick up the receiver and read the instructions on how to dial out. My mind goes blank; I can't remember my dad's phone number. Thankfully I remember my stepmom's; she's had it for the better part of fifteen years. I frantically punch the buttons. They pick up on the second ring. When I hear their voices, I can't help but cry. I explain that Jefferson won't pick me up until Monday, and I'm stuck here.

"I'm terrified," I whisper and sob.

"I know, baby," my dad says.

"Can you pray for me?" I plead.

"I'd be glad to. Lord, I come to You this evening asking for protection over Audrey. Lord, You know Audrey's heart and the fears she has, please wrap Your arms of protection around her as she walks this walk. We may not know the reason why things happen the way they do, but we trust and know that You are in control of all of this. In Your precious name, amen."

14

"Thank you. I'm not sure when I'll be able to talk to you again, but can you please call—"

"You have one minute," a computer automated voice comes on the line.

"Oh gosh, can you call Momma and tell her I'm okay?" frantically thinking of anything else I need to say.

"Yes, we will do that," he says. "We will get you out, just focus on taking care of you, and I'll call Charles to see what we need to do about getting you out."

The line goes dead.

I can't stop crying. They haven't come to get me yet. Who's to say I can't make another phone call?

I pick up the receiver and dial again.

"Hey," my dad answers.

"Thought I'd try again," I quietly say. "Can you also email William? He's my attorney. We've spoken to a criminal lawyer that is familiar with the situation already. You can find his email on my phone." I give him the four-digit code to my phone.

"Yes, give me a minute. I'm writing this down." My dad is working hard to figure out how all this is going to work, and I wish I could hug his neck.

"Thank you," is all I can muster. "I love you, and please

keep praying."

"We will, darlin'."

We hang up, and I wait for the officer to come back for me. Another panic attack takes hold as I try to process everything. Bile rises in my throat, but I refuse to throw up in the clogged toilet, so I move my mind to other things in this room. Fear overcomes me as I read all the pleas and prayers people have scratched on the metal door and walls. Is this the kind of room I'll be in for the next three days? Finally, the door opens, and I wipe the tears off my face. I don't want anyone to see me cry, not here. How brave I think I am.

The door opens, and I'm told, "Put your hands behind your back and wait here," she points against the wall next to another woman inmate who is short and has a mixture of emotions on her face, mostly anger and fear. I worry what kind of people I'll be rooming with. I try to smile at her, but she doesn't look at me.

2

We walk for what seems like ages passing by huge, open rooms with square, gaping windows that resemble exhibits at the zoo. All that's missing is a plaque in front describing the species and wild animals within. Rooms upon rooms of men stare back at us. I try not to look at them for fear. My face reflects how I feel, terrified and weak. We are still on the assembly line, headed to our final destination, our own exhibit. I've always been on the right side of the glass, looking sympathetically at the caged animal. We approach one of the many doors that line the hallway, and the officer rushes her directions. I can hardly keep up with what she's saying.

"Pick up the mattress on top and follow me. Do not pick and choose! Just the one on top."

The other young woman and I quickly scoot in our orange plastic slippers to grab a mattress. I step aside and let her go first. The mattresses, which look like big kindergarten nap mats, are piled on top of each other, forest green plastic. After she moves, my heart sinks as I get a glimpse of which one is next, the one I'm to grab, with rips and flat in the middle where countless other people's hips have eroded what little foam there is inside.

"Hurry up!" The officer yells, and we quicken our pace as we head toward the door. Carrying our awkward mattresses, we finally arrive at what must be the end of the jail where they keep the women. Twenty women stare at us when we walk in the door.

"Tribb, you go to bunk five, Washington, you're at six." We're given single cots on the front row.

The lights are bright fluorescent, and like the men's rooms, there are rows of metal raised beds. There are around thirty metal cots that fill most of the room—bunks in the back, single cots in the front. In the very front of the room, by the square window with the hallway view, are two metal picnic benches on the left and three rows of metal benches for watching the tiny TV near the ceiling.

The heavy metal door slams closed, and I'm overcome with the reality I find myself in. I lay my mattress down on my cot and make my bed with the single sheet, not fitted, and wool blanket covered with holes. I want to sit on my cot and sob. Losing myself right now wouldn't be ideal, but I'm not that far gone yet. I haven't lost all hope.

"I'm Audrey," I say to the girl I came in with.

She stares at me for a minute. Is it a weakness to be nice in here?

Finally, she throws a nod my way and says, "Denisha."

That's where the conversation stops for now, and I'm

okay with that. Not sure I'm ready to talk yet anyway. My mind needs to process next steps. Some women are reading, my favorite thing to do, and I no doubt can pass the time faster that way. Scanning the room, a book laying on a metal box on the wall catches my eye. It's a King James Version Bible, and I thank God for this blessing. The Bible is missing the back pages and is ripped in places, but this tattered book is my confidant now, and I hold it close to my heart.

Now that I'm settled, I sit on my cot and take in my surroundings. I try to organize what belongings I do have: a bar of soap, a less than clean washrag filled with holes, a two-inch-long orange toothbrush, and clear toothpaste in a sugar packet-size container. Although the items are few, I am glad for soap and a toothbrush. Without staring, I attempt to size up the twenty women I'm in here with, most with orange jumpsuits, a few with red, and one with yellow. I wonder whether the different colors signify anything, our very own factions. The woman in yellow seems to be the one in charge as she yells across the room at me that my blanket can't be hanging off the edges of my cot but instead tucked under my mattress. I jump up and do as she says and make sure to thank her. Two women are briskly walking around the room as if it were a track or the mall; I'm assuming to get energy, nervous or otherwise, out that they can't do outside this room.

Most of the women are sitting on their cots talking

to the surrounding others, the alliances they've no doubt already created. The one person I'm even remotely comfortable talking to is Denisha, we came in together, and our beds are next to each other. Like me, she knows no one in here. As soon as I've had this thought, one of the track walkers comes over to Denisha, and they start talking. I have gathered that they are distant cousins. There goes my alliance strategy.

No one talks to me right away, but they are staring. The stares don't make me uncomfortable because they're not filled with hate, more curiosity than anything. I am out-of-place in here, and we all know it. I imagine what they're thinking of me, why I'm here, and what I've done. The story is entirely too long to share with people I will hopefully only know for a brief time. I know the questions are inevitable, so my thoughts travel to how I'm going to answer them.

The sound of a toilet loudly flushing catches me off guard, and I'm brought back to reality. An area to my left is a cement half-wall that hides three metal toilets. Next to the half-wall are three sinks and a water fountain. The mirrors are metal plates screwed into the brick wall that reveal blurred reflections. While the half-wall provides some privacy from the fellow inmates, it leaves nothing for the raised two-way mirrors the officers monitor us through. They will be able to see me every time I use the bathroom. The thought unnerves me and sends a chill down my spine.

"Roll call! Roll call! Roll call!" shouts the muffled speaker.

Everyone jumps up, including those sleeping, straighten their mattresses and belongings, and stand in front of their cot. I follow their lead, hands behind my back, and wait for what I'm not sure. We stand in silence for what feels like an eternity, and my knees are shaking from shock and fear. My body is willing itself to sit, but I remember not to lock my legs, the last thing I want is to pass out right now.

"It's the sergeant!" Someone loudly whispers from the back of the room, and the air becomes tense.

A noise that sounds like high voltage electricity rings in my ear, then the door opens. One officer, and from what I gather, is the sergeant in full police uniform, walks in with a clipboard. She has a scowl on her lightly freckled face, and her black hair is slicked into a strict ponytail, not one hair out of place.

"Give me your full name, bunk number, and absolutely no talking!" she thunders.

She walks through the rows and arrives at me.

"Audrey Tribb, five," I quickly say.

She moves on, and I let out a huge breath I didn't realize I had been holding. No one sits down. How I long to sit down, but I won't be the only one sitting, I must follow everyone else's lead. I'll have to learn the rules and abide by them to survive. *Be invisible, not an inconvenience.*

The only noise in the room is the sergeant walking through the aisles behind me, but I dare not look back. If there ever was a time to play by the rules, it is now. A second door opens in the back, which piques my curiosity. I'll look after she leaves.

"At ease!" she shouts, and movement around the room continues. Now I can sit down. My view turns to the back of the room, where there is another door like ours separating our dormitory area from five individual cells. The sight of these women locked in those cells makes me nervous and glad I'm not locked in there.

I lie down on my cot and pull the wool blanket over me, but the woman in the yellow jumpsuit says we can't until 11:00 tonight. I search the walls for a clock for how many minutes I have left but find none. A new kind of prison, that of uncertainty and days void of time. An unending prison of thought.

The Bible I found is at the foot of my bed and the only solace I can find right now, so I read. In the real world, I too often reach for my phone for distraction. Distraction from my thoughts and things I should be doing. I let the book fall open to a random place, hoping that God would show me what to do. The Bible lands on Psalm 22, a well-worn verse in times of trouble: "My God, My God, why hast thou forsaken me? Why are thou so far from helping me and from the words of my roaring? O my God, I cry in the daytime, but thou hearest not; and in the night season and am not silent."

I forgot how hard the King James Version is to read, but it's my only option, and I can fill my time now with trying to understand it.

Finally, 11:00 must have arrived because the speaker booms, "Lights out!" and a small cheer erupts throughout the room while the women frantically lie down. The lights are only dimmed a fraction that the room is still bright—no other option than to lie down and attempt to sleep. Everyone gets under their covers and stops talking. The silence sets in and is instantly deafening. My thoughts spiral out of control. Ever since I was a child, I needed noise to go to sleep. Are these women able to fall asleep this quickly? Or are they also being tormented by their thoughts? In the worst place, I have found myself, and I long for something to distract my dark and fearful thoughts. I reach for the Bible and read until I fall asleep.

I'm awakened by the door slamming. It doesn't feel like I've been asleep long. I raise my head, squinting the sleep from my eyes. Two new inmates are carrying their mattresses as they head to their assigned bunks. I wish I knew what time it was. Judging by the window on the far side of the room, we are still in the thick of night. My body is violently shaking from what I'm sure is shock. I pick up my Bible in an attempt to keep my mind occupied and try to go back to sleep.

Throughout the night, the guards keep coming in and out as if this were a hospital, and they're checking on their patients, the first oxymoron of this journey. I'd laugh at the thought if the stark reality I find myself in wasn't so dire. The guards don't care about our health or whether we're getting any sleep judging by how hard the door slams. Every time it closes, my body tenses. I've only ever had one panic attack in my life. Now I'm warding them off like wild lions. My mind wonders how one could choose a job like this and whether they're trained to not treat us as humans. Empathy is probably a box that needs to be left unchecked on the application. I am becoming invisible, or maybe they are making me that way, that they don't see me, not because of anything I'm doing, but that I'm just another body to keep track of.

The speaker wakes me with some garbled message I can't understand. A few women wake up and sit on their cots with half-opened eyes.

"What'd they say?" I ask Denisha.

"I dunno," she replies. "Hey Tiffany, what'd they say?" Denisha asks the girl on the back row.

"Breakfast," she groggily says.

The woman in yellow at the back of the room shouts at us, "Get up, ladies, if you want breakfast!"

Typically, I don't eat breakfast, but something tells me

I need to eat something, or at least curiosity gets the best of me, and I pull myself off the cot. I'm not even sure what time it is except for the darkness emitting from the window. Part of me worries the sun won't ever come up again.

The electric volt sounds again, and the door opens. Two men in matching yellow jumpsuits push a tall cart with rows of tan trays. A guard grabs four trays and hands four cups to the woman in yellow. They walk to the back where the individual cells are and distribute the food to the four women. When they come out, the woman in yellow shouts, "Ladies, get in line if you want breakfast!" She's very comfortable with the guards and seems too at home here.

Only six of us grab a tray and sit on the metal benches as we look at what they've served us. Something begins to rise in my throat, bile, I'm sure. But instead, what comes up surprises me and everyone at the table. A sob escapes my mouth as if it were vomit, and I cry like I never have before. It's the most out of control I've felt in my entire life. I half-wished that when I woke up, it'd all been a horrific nightmare. That fleeting moment lasted only seconds when I woke and forgot about what happened the day before, and then the reality engulfed me. I guess I'm still swallowed whole by it. It's not the food I'm crying about, although the look of it does make me nauseous. A rubber-looking piece of sausage, ten pieces of canned pineapple, a square piece of thick bread that resembles cornbread, and a doughy pan-

25

cake with no syrup or butter. The women at the table don't acknowledge me at all.

"I'll take your sausage if you're not going to eat it," mumbles Tiffany with food in her mouth.

"Yeah, I'll take your cake," pipes in her friend.

The cake must be the cornbread-looking thing. I slide my tray over, and they quickly grab up what they can. The woman in yellow comes over to take the pancake. Their behavior toward this tasteless food is the most bizarre thing I've ever seen. Ravenous wolves taking what they can before someone else does. A live-action picture of survival. Animalistic. They must have seen my look of disdain and nausea. I worry they'll think I'm some weak, spoiled brat. They don't seem to mind my disdain for the food, after all, it's more food for them. Suppressing my thoughts and utter sadness, I think I have to be stronger to survive this. Snap out of it and get it together.

"Where can I get a cup?" I ask no one in particular. I've seen cups sitting on their cots, and I desperately need water.

"Next time we eat, ask the guard for a cup," Tiffany tells me with her mouth half-full of chewed-up meat.

Next time we eat? That must be around lunchtime. I must think for myself and at least five steps ahead. But that's not me. I'm not calculating. What you see is what you get. Instead, the water fountain will have to do for now and appease my thirst. After clearing their trays in the trash, the women head back to their cots and under their blankets. I realize that I need to take this opportunity to go to the bathroom while everyone is lying down.

After lining the seat with toilet paper, I unbutton the silver buttons on my jumpsuit. Thankfully I have a T-shirt underneath, so I'm not completely topless, small victories I hold dear in here. What is life if you don't have hope? Even hope as small as this. I grip the top of my jumpsuit on both sides so it doesn't touch the floor. My eyes scan the room and realize my previous observations were right: the guard window reveals a full view of the toilets for the guards to see over the half-wall. I hurry and finish.

My mind is going ninety miles an hour which only speeds up my heart rate and further frays my nerves. The soft sounds of the inmates breathing don't provide relief from the deafening voices shouting insults of shame in my head. Reaching down, I do the only thing that quiets me and pick up the Bible I've laid under my cot. I turn again to Psalms. When my company started to unravel three months ago, I began to identify with David, the small shepherd boy turned king. Like David, I found myself in a wilderness. This time I read Psalm 23. I know there's no coincidence that the spine of the book automatically opens to this page. Many inmates have found comfort in this well-worn page, and I join them as I read, but this time I, like many inmates before, cling to verses 4 and 5: "Yea though I walk through the valley of the shadow of death, I will fear no evil: for thou art with me; thy rod and thy staff they comfort me. Thou preparest a table before me in the presence of mine enemies: thou anointest my head with oil; my cup runneth over."

I will fear no evil, I silently repeat to myself. As I close my eyes, I pray the simplest prayer I can, "Lord, please protect me and provide peace that passes all understanding." Silently, I cry myself to sleep.

3

"Roll call! Roll call! Roll call!" the speaker blasts over the quiet. It doesn't take much to wake me from my fitful sleep. Reality doesn't escape me even in sleep, the conscious world ever-present in my dream world. I sit up on my 4" mattress and begin to make my bed, following the lead of the others. We all stand at the end of our cots and wait.

Buzz. The door opens, and in walks a heavy-set man in his 50s accompanied by our shift officer. He gives his directions on how roll call works then ambles to the front row. As he makes his way through the inmates, he stops in front of me.

"Audrey Tribb, bunk five," I stammer.

He seems as if he's assessing me. I'm not sure whether to look at him or not. So I give my best Audrey smile. He doesn't smile back and thankfully continues his inmate checks. Why did I smile? I silently argue with myself while he continues his checks. My thoughts begin to race. He didn't stop in front of anyone else, and I'm not the only new one here. Maybe I look out of place, or maybe he knows the man who put me here. Either way, it doesn't sit well with me. A dark feeling creeps up my spine and settles in my chest.

"At ease, ladies," he says finally as he heads for the door.

Exhausted, I sit on my cot and open my Bible to Psalms again. I begin to understand the insanity of being in this place, and I've not been here twelve hours. The mind can be a trap and the worst place to be stuck. No distractions. The only thing keeping me company are my thoughts, and they're not friendly. *I'm sitting in jail*, I think as I look down at this horrendous orange canvas I'm wearing. I see myself as that sergeant did, as I'm sure my parents do, and the other inmates. How could I ever have thought I was special?

Shame rears its ugly head and engulfs me. It's a funny thing, shame. Before you can recognize what it is, it's wrapped its vine-like tentacles throughout your body, piercing your soul in tiny jabs first, then later sharp, decisive cuts. It grows in a way I never thought possible, that most people don't, I'm sure, as it begins to fill every fiber of my being. Shame like I've never felt before. The more I water this shame vine, the faster it grows, penetrating the cracks that were already there, splintering me into a thousand pieces. It's not a coincidence that shame and Satan are both five-letter words. I know the truth, but it feels like everyone else doesn't. They see a mugshot and, as a jury of one determine guilt, because you can't be arrested if you're not guilty right? Will my friends and family believe me that this is a huge mistake? A misunderstanding? Do they trust in who they know me to be?

"What time do the phones turn on?" I hear Denisha ask Tiffany.

"8:00," replies Tiffany.

I nearly jump off my cot, frantically searching the room for a phone. Two phones sit on the wall in the back of the room. I've never been happier in my entire life. How did I not see those last night? We don't have a clock, but we do have access to the outside world. Voices from home. Familiar voices that will carry me through the day.

Tiffany teaches me how to use the phone by using the numbers on my inmate bracelet, and I quickly dial my stepmom's phone number. The phone seems to ring for ages. No answer. My heart sinks. I dial my mom. Thankfully, the automated voice says, "Please hold while the person you are calling is entering information to accept your call." Relief floods my body.

"Hey, sweetie," my mom's soft voice comes on the line.

Hearing her voice is so soothing I can't help but cry. I wanted to be strong for her, to not have her bear the pain of hearing me so fragile and weak, but the familiarity of hearing her say my name reminds me who I am.

"Momma, I'm so scared. I can't process any of this. How did all this happen?"

"Oh honey, I'm so sorry." She sounds like she's holding back her own tears, trying to be strong for me.

"Did Daddy call you?" I ask.

"Yes, he called me last night." My initial thought is how awkward that conversation must've been. They haven't exchanged more than mere pleasantries at graduations and birthday parties for the last two decades. For a moment, I'm proud of them for putting their differences aside and parenting their twenty-eight-year-old independent child. The shame vine grows a little more with this thought.

"I tried calling them, but they didn't answer. What all did he say?"

The automated operator comes on the line, "You have one minute."

"Did you hear that?" We ask simultaneously. Momma and I have always been in sync. We are nearly the same person. All her eccentricities and things that annoy her were passed down to me. People chewing is at the top of the list. I'm most proud to have gotten her ability to unconditionally love. When she loves you, she does it fiercely and relentlessly. When she and daddy split, it broke my heart. Not in the way you'd imagine divorce to affect a child, obviously the hurt was unreal at the beginning. Kids are resilient, but I didn't realize until the past few years how it had changed me all those years ago. Every now and then, I'll look at the photo albums that used to hold our whole family. Missing pictures on each page clearly where momma used to be. My brain is against me now while it's empty of thought. I need to stop thinking of the past and focus on what lies ahead.

"I think I'll try to call daddy back to see what they've found out," I reply.

"Okay, you can call me anytime. I'll have my phone on me. I think I need to set up an account, so we can talk longer," she says.

"I love you, Momma. I'm sorry about all this," I say in the strongest voice I can muster.

"Please don't apologize. I know what really happened. I don't have the kind of money you need for bail, but I can help in any other way if you need me. You just have to tell me."

"Yes, ma'am, please pray for me."

"I have all night and will continue to." My heart aches that I've put my family in this position. This was my mistake, not theirs.

I hang up before the operator decides when my call ends. Control is what I've always liked best, so if deciding when I hang up the phone is the smallest bit of control I have, I'll take it.

This time my stepmom picks up, and I can tell I'm on speaker. Both my dad and stepmom are listening. I've only heard my dad cry twice in my life—when my grandfather passed away and today.

"I've called all my sisters to pray for you. They are prayer warriors and are lifting you up." A guttural sob escapes him. The sound shocks my system. I can't hold back anymore. I've caused him this pain, and my heart aches that he is so sad because of me. We cry together for a moment.

"Will you pray for me?" I quietly ask. Ever since I was little, I watched in awe of my dad's walk with Christ. He was a leader in our small-town church, tithed his 10 percent without fail, and always told me to do the right thing. If ever there was a man who walked closely with God, it was this one, and I thankfully get to ask him to pray over me. A direct line to God, I felt.

"I'd be glad to. Dear Jesus, we know that You are in control of this situation. Lord, nothing takes You by surprise, and although we don't have all the answers right now, we know that You have Audrey in the palm of Your hand. We have prayers going up across the nation for my girl, and I know You love her more than I could. I thank You for what You've already done and that You will continue to protect her. In Your heavenly and glorious name. Amen."

The line is quiet after he finishes, and I'm not sure what to say. The vine of shame wraps around me, squeezing.

"Thank you, Daddy. They say Jefferson won't pick me up until Monday. This is the loneliest place I've ever been, and most hours, I feel I won't make it."

"You will, baby. You'll get through this. I'll call Charles and see about getting you out of Jefferson on Monday. Let's take this one step at a time. I've already emailed your attorney and let him know you've been picked up."

"Did he email you back?" I ask.

"Yes, he said he'd be in contact with the criminal attorney to discuss what they could do," he replies.

"Okay, thank you. I'm sorry you had to see all that last night," I say.

"We'll get through this," he says.

We hang up, and I head back to my cot.

"Were you able to talk to your family?" Denisha asks as she fixes her hair back into a small ponytail.

"Yeah. What about you?"

"My baby daddy's keeping my four-month-old, and he won't pick up the phone. I know he alright, I jus' worry, ya know?" A tear creeps out of her eye, so I do my best to sound sympathetic.

"Man, that's rough. Can you bond out?" I ask.

"They picked me up for traffic tickets. 'Failure to yield,' and apparently, my driver's license is expired. My lil' sheet of paper says 'No bond' for the failure to yield. How can

35

you arrest me on traffic tickets? I better be home by Christmas." I envy her confidence.

"I didn't know they could either."

A voice from the back says in our direction, "They're on a warrant spree, tryin' to pick everyone up before the holidays."

The thought of the holidays makes my stomach turn. One thing you can forget in here—no decorations, no trees, no Christmas spirit. Cold concrete box with metal beds replaces any warmth of softness the holidays bring.

Thankfully, Denisha interrupts my thoughts, "Why you in here?"

I give a half-laugh and sigh, "Where do I start?" I take a deep breath and do my best to explain, "I own an interior design company, and my business partner didn't have the license she thought she did. One of my clients found out the same time I did and used it to her advantage. She then called my other clients and had them file charges against me. It's a nightmare." There it is, hanging in the air. Saying it out loud sounds ridiculous. I gauge their reactions, not knowing them makes it harder to know how they'll react. I wait.

Finally, Denisha is the first to speak, "They can file criminal charges against you for that?" Tiffany walks over to listen, apparently intrigued. I'm sure they all want to know why I'm here.

"I guess so, they're felony charges, they're calling it fraud. I've only been in business a year. My attorney said, 'You may be stupid, but you're not a criminal.' I wish my clients saw it that way, but she's looking to not pay the money she owes me." For the first time, I look them in the face.

"That's wild," Tiffany says as she takes a seat on the cot behind me, genuinely interested.

"The worst part is, one of my clients is a New Orleans police officer, a lieutenant at that. So, being in here, in his territory, terrifies me."

"No way!" Denisha gasps.

"You got a good lawyer, though, don't you?" Tiffany quickly asks.

"Yeah, and my dad is helping to figure all this out." I might have it a lot better than most of these women in here who probably don't have help, and the last thing I want to do is come off as arrogant.

"Well, that's good," Tiffany clicks her tongue ring.

"Why are you here?" I ask Tiffany, trying to redirect the conversation away from me.

"I got in trouble while on parole. Here until January 9th. Got a seven-year-old at home."

"Boy or girl?" I ask.

"Lil' boy."

"Are you able to talk to him?" I don't want to upset her.

"He's stayin' with my mom, I talk to him sometimes. Jus' too hard most days."

"At least they answer the phone. My baby daddy betta answer that phone next time I call. I'm so mad," Denisha says as she stands up to make another phone call.

Tiffany and I sit in awkward silence now that Denisha is gone. I noticed a book on her cot last night, so I attempt to make small talk.

"What are you reading?" I nod over at the book on her cot.

"Oh, the Bible. It's hard to read."

"Yeah, I thought the same thing. Some things make sense. It keeps my mind busy and encourages me, but praying is what gets me through."

"Me too."

"How long have you been in here?" I ask her quietly.

"Since December 8th."

She's a veteran in here, I assume then. Her hair is dyed maroon, almost hot pink. She must be in her early 20s, and she's tall and slim. Her jumpsuit actually fits her, while I look like a toddler in mommy's nightshirt.

"Do they turn the TV on at all?" I ask her. I noticed it last night and was relieved for another distraction.

"Yeah, around 10:00 if they feel like it. We watch movies and a lot of trashy reality shows," she laughs.

Movement catches my eye from the corner of the room. The woman in yellow grabs a deck of cards and sits down to play solitaire. By the look of her bun, she has long, dark hair. She's tall too and thirty-something. Her pile of hair sits directly on top of her head, making her tiny frame look like it's struggling to hold it all up. She walks around with a sense of authority. The criminal room mom. She knows all the rules and makes sure we abide by them, probably not to forfeit any freedoms for her or ourselves. Any kind of authority given in a place like this can be dangerous; I try to keep this in the back of my mind.

Tiffany sees me staring at the woman in yellow, "Steer clear of that one," she says in a whisper.

"Oh, why's that?" I ask her quietly.

"She alone a lot, talks to herself, and laughs like she crazy. No one knows why she here. I jus' don't trust people like that."

"Thanks for the heads up."

Tiffany gets up and heads for the toilet. Alone again, my thoughts begin to retrace all that led up to this point. It was September when I found out the license was wrong.

A month later, the state gave us the right license. I thought that would have been the end of it. The government entity that grants the licenses gave me the right one. One plus one doesn't always equal two, apparently. I've corrected the license issue, lost thousands of dollars in attorney fees and deals lost. The bank shut my funding down, and my new clients couldn't afford to wait on me to get this sorted out—what a mess. I never knew that it'd get this far.

4

A tiny, older woman with a few missing teeth and a shaved head comes to sit by Denisha's bunk. When she got out of bed this morning, I caught a glimpse of her kneeling in prayer. This is a woman I want to trust, but for now, I fall asleep listening to them talk. Comfort can be found in the strangest places, and right now, knowing I'm not alone and the proximity of their voices puts me to sleep. For whatever reason, I trust them.

I wake to the sound of the TV and the guard asking what channel we want to watch. Finally, something to distract my thoughts for a while. They begin to shout, "Bravo!" "FX!" "BET!" They ultimately settle on FX. Hearing them reach an agreement is nothing but irony. They began a polite war, "No, it's okay, we can watch Bravo," "FX is fine. I don't really care." This moment is when I began to realize that these are people like me—people. People who've made mistakes but don't have the resources to help themselves. People who have worries and no money to make bail or no transportation for their family to get here. Or no family at all.

I lay there and watch the TV. Luckily my bunk has a direct shot of the 28" TV. The speaker shouts its grainy command again, "Roll call! Roll call! Roll call!"

Groans can be heard throughout the room as we all get up and stand in front of our cots. They left the TV on so at least I can watch while standing and waiting. A fanged joker comes across the screen, and I slowly realize this is a horror movie.

"What movie is this?" I turn to quietly ask Denisha.

"Ugh, *Malpus*. I hated this movie when I was a kid."

"I've never heard of it. What is it?"

"It's a scary Christmas movie," she replies.

A scary Christmas movie? If ever there was a definition of oxymoron, then it'd be this. Why would anyone make a Christmas horror movie? I learned later it's about a demon named Malpus. The devil is afoot, especially in jail, where loneliness, hopelessness, and depression abide. My previous luck of being close to the TV has now turned to misfortune. With shame, I bow my head and wait for the sergeant to finish roll call.

Throughout the day, I alternate calling my mom and dad every hour. It's the only time I cry. Hearing their voices reminds me how far away they are, but I need to hear them. They pray over me every time we talk, and this is getting me through the day. I sit at the table and read my Bible while *Malpus* is on the TV. A woman in her 40s sits across from me. She's slept most of the day. They bring her medicine every four hours.

"I'm Robin," she says as she tousles her short, dyed blond hair.

"Hey, I'm Audrey."

"You doin' okay?" she asks.

I'm taken aback by this, so it takes me a minute to respond.

"I'm okay, best I can be, I guess."

"That's good. You bondin' out today?" her southern accent drawls.

"No, ma'am, I'm waiting on Jefferson to pick me up, then I have to go to St. Charles."

"Girl, what did you do?"

I retell the story to her. I watch her reaction, but she's probably the type of person who isn't surprised by anything. Tattoos peek out under the arms of her jumpsuit and travel down her forearms. Her fingernails are dirty, and her eyes look tired. This isn't her first time in jail.

"Yeah, I'm waiting on my bond to be paid here, then I gotta go to Texas."

"Do you mind me asking why you're here?"

"A stupid mistake. I stole a drill," she gives a throaty laugh.

"A Christmas gift?" I ask her.

She nods as she rubs her arm and yawns.

"These pills they're givin' me make me so dang sleepy. I'm not gonna take 'em anymore," she says resolutely. She's using what little control she has. I find myself wishing for something to make me sleep the days away.

"I haven't always been this way. I started using drugs only five years ago. Meth. Then I met a man who beat on me. I'm with a good guy now, though. He's tryin' to borrow money to get me outta here."

"I hope he can get it paid today and that you're home for Christmas. That's all I'm hoping for," I trail off.

"Yeah, I got grandbabies…" she can't finish as she wipes her eyes.

"I'll pray for you," I tell her.

"Thanks."

She must've had enough because she lies back down on her cot. I like her, though. She's motherly and confident. The type to take care of whoever she's with, loyal. I say a silent prayer for her.

The speaker sends out another garbled message. I see the woman in yellow get up and begin to put black rubber gloves on.

"Lunch time, ladies!" she yells.

Finally, a cup. After distributing lunch to the cells in the back, we line up for our trays. Macaroni noodles with blocks of ham (or is it spam?), corn, three lemon sandwich cookies, and more cornbread. What is the deal with all this bread? Much like breakfast, my stomach turns, and I swallow down the bile. I grab the cookies and slide my tray to let the wolves descend. They eat as they've never eaten before.

"I can't," I mumble.

"You eat, or you starve," one of the women says with a mouth full of macaroni.

She's not wrong, but the smell emanating from that ham tells everything in my body not to eat it. I won't starve on day one. My thoughts are interrupted by commotion at the next table.

"That should be illegal! I can't finish my food now!" Tiffany shouts with her mouth full of macaroni, pointing behind me.

Everyone turns around to see what she's talking about. In one of the back cells stands a robust woman completely naked. I'm shocked by the sight and turn away immediately.

"She on suicide watch. That's why she only got that lil' cover," someone says.

45

They start to laugh and make jokes about not being able to finish lunch, and I can't help but laugh too. It feels good to laugh, although part of me feels guilty for having joy or poking fun at her. I take my cup and cookies in a brown paper towel and go back to my cot. They turned the TV off during lunch. I have mixed feelings, glad that awful movie is off, but now there's nothing to distract me.

As the hours drag on, my head begins to pound, and I get a headache so awful it feels it might split in two. At first, I think I'm dehydrated, but then I realize I haven't had coffee. Oh, no, no medicine, and I doubt they'll give me anything. My thoughts turn to medicine, and I try to remember what date it is. I begin to panic. I'm supposed to start any day, and I don't have any medicine. My endometriosis causes my period to be so painful I have to go to the ER if I don't have my medicine. While I realize it's the strangest prayer I've ever prayed, I do it anyway. I pray for a delay. Please, Jesus, I won't survive the pain if I don't have medicine.

Shortly after lunch, they turn the TV back on, and this time an action movie is on. I can deal with this. A buff, meaty guy is refreshing compared to the awful scenes of *Malpus*. My body begins to ache from this metal cot and the tension I keep in my muscles. The entire room is hard, full of metal and concrete. What little softness I have is my mattress and blanket. Exhaustion overwhelms me, and sleep evades me. I need to save sleep for tonight anyway.

Behind me, I hear someone struggling to breathe. I turn and see it's one of the new inmates who came in the middle of the night.

"Are you okay?" I ask her.

She nods her head, then walks to the intercom. I can't hear the exchange, but she walks back to her bed visibly in distress. Her wheezing has become worse as she plops down on her cot.

I begin to worry about her and the obvious distress she is in. I feel helpless as I hear her gasp for air. She walks back to the intercom, and again I can't make out what's said. Still, no one comes to help her.

Not knowing what to do, I decide to be bold and walk over to her, doing the only thing I know how.

"Can I sit down?" I quietly ask.

She nods her head again, and I sit next to her.

"Do you mind if I pray for you?"

Her eyes look at me in desperation, and I take that as a yes. I wrap my arm around her and begin to pray for her.

"Dear God, we come to You in our moment of distress. I ask that You, the Great Physician, put healing on this woman's body and let her lungs take in the air she desper-ately needs. Please calm her spirits and give her peace that only You can provide. We thank You for what You've already done. In Your precious name, Amen."

After I open my eyes, I see that she's silently crying. I give her one big squeeze and let go. Finally, the door opens, and a guard walks in with what appears to be a breathing machine. Her body relaxes in relief as she walks over to the guard and plugs in the machine. I silently thank God for this blessing and head back to lie down. The sound of the breathing machine lulls me into a restless sleep.

5

The rest of the day goes by much the same, sleep, watch TV, read, then eat supper—spaghetti with green beans and cornbread. I take a few bites of spaghetti which isn't as awful as the macaroni ham we had for lunch. My leftovers were quickly devoured by those sitting near me. I notice that they've left the back door open that separates our room from the individual cells.

"Why are they in there?" I ask anyone at the table.

"They were prolly actin' crazy when they were arrested. Fightin' and stuff," one of the other women, who I now know as Sofia, answers.

Sofia's face matches her personality, childlike. She's been sitting on one of the front benches nearly the whole day watching TV. She laughs at almost everything, and her joy is sometimes contagious. Her orange jumpsuit swallows her tiny frame. Too many cigarettes have left her voice deep and raspy, a contrast to the rest of her. She does look like she's been through a lot. Life has dealt some blows, and I don't know her, but it's apparent in her expressions and bags under her eyes.

"How long have you been here?" I ask her.

"December 12th, doin' stupid stuff," she replies like she knows my follow-up question. Same conversations, different people. The obligatory introductory conversation that's now a rite of passage amongst the inmates.

"When can you get out?"

"Not until January 17th." Her eyes seem far away.

I don't know what to say because no amount of empathy I can offer will take her out of this place.

"I seen you prayin' for that woman earlier," she continues.

My heart begins to pound, worried which way this is going to go.

"Can you pray for me sometime?" she asks.

Relief floods me, "I'd love to do that. After we eat, we can pray if you like."

"That'd be good, thank you," she says.

As everyone finishes their tray, I begin to watch the woman in yellow. I've heard her talking to herself like Tiffany said. She generally keeps to herself. Her cot is in the back corner, and she's slept most of the day. I overheard her say she took two Benadryl. I desperately need something for this headache, and the idea that she has Benadryl gives me hope that I can have Tylenol.

Three lemon cookies and water in hand, I head to my cot while I wait for Sofia to finish eating. She's one that eats so fast and asks for everyone else's food. She seems starved. After I left the table, I saw her and Tiffany whispering, hoping they're not making fun of me or plotting something against me. Instead, I'm surprised when Tiffany and Sofia come over to me when they're done and say that they've talked to some other women and they'd like me to lead them in a prayer circle this evening before bed.

"Yes!" I could barely contain my excitement. Maybe this is why God wants me here. My light is shining bright for all to see and God is helping and protecting me. A week ago, a small voice whispered to me, "But what if I ask you to go, Audrey?" I knew it was God, and the thought terrified me. I ignored it, and it asked me again and again. Eventually, I replied very hesitantly, "God, if that is what You will for me to do and You are going to protect me, then I'll go. You know how scared I am. Please don't leave me." A week later, I was arrested.

In July, when the license was found to be wrong, the reaction of my clients was the most surprising. It was like something switched in them. Turns out the woman behind this whole thing, Ms. Broussard, called the state to have them investigate. No one ever called me. No one asked me any questions, the warrants were set, and I was deemed a fraud. I had a license; it just was the wrong one. Couldn't they see that? What do they say? Ignorance isn't an excuse in the eyes of the law. What happens if they are constantly changing the law? They changed this law two short years ago. I'm beginning to learn how broken our justice system is, especially in Louisiana. We are always the last to the table.

All those months ago, when my business partner called me and said the investigator was calling me a thief and that I had gone on some extravagant vacation, I panicked. Where was she getting this information? And who would be lying about stuff like this? I got her phone number and called immediately.

"Sandy Colefield, Investigations," she answered quickly and already sounded irritated.

"Hi, yes, this is Audrey Tribb with Magnolia Maison. My business partner, Allie, said I need to contact you regarding our license."

"Oh, okay. Yes, it looks like you're in violation of the statute RS 37:3176. You are practicing with the wrong certification. You need to have passed the NCIDQ exam," she says sternly.

"I had no idea. I would like to apologize, this was not on purpose, and we already sent in our application for the new license to correct the issue," I said sweetly.

"Ma'am, all that matters is that you were advertising your interior design services and entering into contracts as an interior designer, and you are not licensed to be one," she curtly replies.

"Yes, ma'am, we do have a license. We didn't know it was the wrong one. I now realize our error, but we are trying to rectify the situation immediately," I try to remain calm, but her tone and attitude are beginning to frustrate me.

"To be frank, *ma'am*," she nearly spits the last part out, "the warrants have already been issued, and the statute has been met, you might want to contact my detective friend. I'll send you his number."

"Wait, warrants? Like arrest warrants?"

"Yes," her voice is harsh.

"I also wanted to ask about why you called my business partner and myself thieves."

She sounds irritated. "I told her what the *definition* of a thief was."

"But Ms. Broussard owes us money. How can I be a thief if she hasn't paid me? In this case, wouldn't she be the thief?"

This seems to take her back, and she's speechless for a moment. It appears I now know where the lies are coming from, so while I have her attention, I ask the second question.

"Allie also told me that you said something about me taking a $30,000 vacation."

"I never said that," she quickly quips.

"I've known Allie my entire life; she wouldn't lie to me."

"All I'm saying is that the statute has been met, and the warrants are active."

"Are you saying I can go to jail?"

"I'm saying you can be *arrested*."

Her statement hangs in the air as my mind begins to spin. Why would she say it like that? Like I can't go to jail, just be arrested. I make a mental note to mull this over later.

"Did the State Board file these charges against us?" I ask her.

"No, we don't file charges, we distribute fines and do our best to stay neutral. And to be clear, the warrant is against you since you were the one who signed the contracts."

I try to maintain my composure as she says this, it sounds like Ms. Broussard has gotten in her ear, and Ms. Colefield hasn't given us a fair or unbiased investigation.

"But this is my first time talking to you, and it sounds like the investigation is already done. Do I not have any rights? I thought the Board was also in the business of protecting me as a business owner."

"The statute has been met, it's black and white," she firmly states. "Please seriously consider contacting my detective friend," she continues.

As we hang up, I can't help but replay her words in my head, "You can be *arrested.*" What a weird way for her to phrase that. She corrected me about going to jail. Arrested, not jail. Why would that exist? What would be the point of getting arrested then? Is this something you can't be convicted of? The questions keep coming with no apparent answers.

I do a quick internet search of Sandy Colefield. The results bring up her LinkedIn profile, "Sandra J. Colefield, Compliance Investigator for the Louisiana State Board of Interior Designers." I'm shocked when I see her location, "Covington Area." The same location Ms. Broussard lives. But I guess that's why she was assigned Ms. Broussard's case. The thought still makes me apprehensive. They're from the same neck of the woods.

My mind is racing as I search through the Board's website, looking for what I'm not sure. I stumbled upon Robert Thompson's name. Apparently, he's the Compliance Director. I'm assuming Sandy Colefield's boss. I decide to rip the band-aid off and call him. I have to try to get ahead of this, although it feels I'm already behind.

"Good afternoon, this is Rob," he answers on the first ring.

Part of me thought I'd get his voicemail, and now I don't know where to start.

"Hi, um, Mr. Thompson, this is Audrey Tribb out of New Orleans with Magnolia Maison."

"Hi, Ms. Tribb. What can I do for you today?" He sounds chipper for the moment.

"Well, I'm not quite sure where to start. I just got off the phone with Ms. Colefield out of St. Tammany parish," I pause to see if he knows who I'm referencing.

"Mm-hmm," he responds.

Good, I think he knows her. "She said there are arrest warrants out for me for having the wrong license. We tried to fix the situation immediately and sent a new application in when we realized, but now I fear it's too late."

"You said arrest warrants?" he asks.

"Yes, Ms. Colefield said the Board doesn't file charges, but there's no way Ms. Broussard knew the law without Ms. Colefield's guidance, who ironically also encouraged me to contact her detective *friend*." I emphasize friend, so he understands my meaning.

I can hear him take a deep breath, "Well, it sounds like you don't need to speak to Ms. Colefield anymore. Please direct any future questions to me. Listen, we are in the business of getting you your license, that's our whole purpose. We want you to have it."

He sounds genuine in his response which makes me relieved and that maybe the Board can help.

"I read online that I might need to cease and desist operations while I wait for the correct license."

"Yes, if you give me your email, I'll send you the cease-and-desist letter."

It sounds as though the Board is playing catch up as well. Why would warrants already be issued, but I haven't even been given a cease and desist? This is spinning out of control while Sandy Colefield and Ms. Broussard are at the wheel.

"Does the Board file criminal charges against interior designers?" I continue trying to make sense of this.

"No, we only determine if a license needs to be revoked, an interior designer needs to cease-and-desist operations, or we fine the interior designer. Mainly situations like yours result in a fine."

"You're telling me that the Board will most likely fine me, yet the law considers this a felony? The Board is the one handing out the licenses. How can this be so upside down?" I say, struggling to remain calm.

"That's just the way it is, Ms. Tribb." I can tell he doesn't want to talk anymore, so I decide to wrap it up with him and not push my luck.

"I appreciate your information. Do you mind if I call you back for any other questions I might have?"

He sighs, "Sure. You can also email me."

"Okay, thank you."

"You have two options, Audrey," begins Mr. Westwood. Paul Westwood sits across from Allie and me at the long conference table. He's one of New Orleans' best criminal attorneys that William, my attorney, brought in to consult us on what to do. He's tall and walks with an air about him that exudes confidence. It intimidates me. He's nice but blunt and wasting no time.

"Try to settle this thing out with Ms. Broussard and your attorney. Or you can turn yourself in, and I can take your case on for $25,000 to make this thing go away."

"I'm supposed to go to my cousin's wedding in Arkansas this weekend," is all I can say. My brain won't keep up. I don't have $25,000, and I'm determined to get my money back from Ms. Broussard.

William interrupts my thoughts, "Listen, why don't you

go to your cousin's wedding and let me reach out to Ms. Broussard's attorney and see what kind of settlement we can come up with."

He knows I don't have that kind of money, and I don't want to turn myself in. We've spent the last couple of months going over my contracts, making sure they were impenetrable. Neither one of us saw this coming. He's a general business attorney, and I'm sure he doesn't know much about the law when it comes to interior design.

"Make sure to set your cruise control and stop at all stop signs. If you get arrested, make sure to let me know, and I'll get you out," Mr. Westwood half laughs.

It's just another case to him. This is my life, but I have full confidence that we can reach an agreement while I'm out of town. Quick and semi-painless. I'll email from the road and reach an agreement quickly, so I don't get arrested.

Mr. Westwood leaves, and William asks what my settlement terms are for Ms. Broussard.

"I definitely want my money back. And obviously, have these charges dropped. I can't believe she can press criminal charges on something like this," I say, still in shock.

"How much money do you have into the project?"

"$58,000." Verbalizing the amount makes it real. I know I won't get the full amount, and the thought sickens me. Not only is she trying to get me arrested, but she's also trying to take my money on the project she already had unpaid upgrades for. She found a loophole and is taking complete advantage of the situation. When we signed the contract nearly six months ago, she was so excited. We agreed that God had brought us together. We hugged and cried because I was getting to start my business, and she was excited about her brand-new home. I didn't think people actually did stuff like this; little did I know this was only the beginning.

"Audrey?" I didn't realize William had been talking to me.

"I'm sorry, what did you say?" I ask.

"I'll email Ms. Broussard's attorney asking what her settlement terms are. Anything I receive, I'll forward to you, and let's go from there, okay?"

"Okay," I quietly reply.

"In the meantime, go on your trip and let me know if any new developments happen, and I'll do the same."

6

"I could scream. This aggravates me so much. I can only imagine how you feel, but it makes me want to punch Ms. Broussard in the nose," my mom says as she clenches her fists. Her statement surprises me. My mom is the least violent person you'd meet. I get my people-pleasing tendencies from her, but it also makes me proud. She truly sees this was an honest mistake. "Why would anyone want you arrested? How can they do that?" she continues.

"I don't want to add any stress to your plate, Momma. It sounds like William has it under control for now and will try to have this settled before I go back home."

"Oh sweetheart, I just don't understand people. Even though you're twenty-eight, you're still my daughter, and I want to protect you," she noticeably relaxes, but you can tell her pain hasn't eased by the faraway look her eyes still hold. I couldn't imagine having a daughter whom I couldn't protect in her adult life. I heard somewhere that when you have kids, it's like having your heart walking outside of your body, vulnerable.

"I know. Let's focus on the wedding festivities for now and enjoy our time together," I say as I squeeze her hand.

My mom and stepdad flew in from Colorado for the

wedding. We've lived without each other since I was in 6th grade, but that's a different story for a different day. We talk every couple of days, mostly about what's going on with me, how incredibly selfish that sounds. So often, we are blinded by our own trials that we forget to ask about the people we love most.

"What time is the rehearsal dinner tonight?" I ask her, trying to refocus her attention.

"Mia said to be at the lake house at 6:45." The tactic works because she picks up her makeup bag and heads for the mirror.

While she's occupied, I check my email for any updates from William. Nothing. Not knowing what to expect, I'm half relieved nothing shows up. At least I won't have to deal with it tonight, and my anxiety dissipates.

The rehearsal dinner momentarily takes my mind off my current troubles. My mom and I agreed not to share any information yet for several reasons. Mostly because I didn't want to dampen Mia's weekend and because I didn't want to have to explain how complicated this all was to the *whole* family. Mainly, I was embarrassed. A year ago, I was so proud of myself for branching out and taking a risk. Now I feel all the "I told you so's" will come in an onslaught. They've already been flooding my mind. I'm not ready for them to come from actual people yet.

Families in the south are more direct but in a round-about, more passive-aggressive way. Only older, southern women can get away with saying things like, "See, that's why I always stayed home" or "That's why when you begin with a company, you retire with that company." Everyone always joked those good southern girls go to college to get an MRS degree, but we all knew it was mostly true. Well, it's not like that anymore. At least I never dreamed of it being that way. I've always wanted to work for myself and wanted so badly to succeed and prove myself. Now, I feel like I'm running with my tail tucked between my legs, ful-filling every undercut they throw my way.

As if she can read my thoughts, my aunt bursts into my thoughts, "How's that interior design thing going, Audrey?"

"It's good, Aunt Carolyn. Going through the first year growing pains, trying to figure it all out," I try to be vague, honest, and nondescript all at once.

"How's...oh, I can never remember her name," Aunt Carolyn struggles.

"Allie? She's good, maintaining the business while I'm away," I quickly respond, hoping this ends soon.

"That's good. Well, you know we're so proud of you." I half-wonder whether she'd say that if she really knew the ghastly truth that a member of her family had an arrest warrant, let alone a girl in her family. I know she's filling the dead air with empty conversation. Shame lifts its ugly head again, taunting me. Will I find support during this? Maybe to my face, but I'm sure side conversations will hold the darker truths, their real thoughts.

My phone dings its signature incoming email alert. Aunt Carolyn walks away, assuming we're done talking since I grab my phone. I sit down at the table nearest me, my heart lurches into my stomach as I read the subject from William: "Broussard: Settlement." Apprehensively I open and quickly scan the message:

Audrey,

Sorry, it's so late, but I just got word from Ms. Broussard's attorney. Ms. Broussard states that she will not drop the charges and will not pay the full sum of $58,000. I requested Quantum Merit for the work completed, and at first, her attorney agreed to this and even advised Ms. Broussard of the law of Quantum Merit. Still, she is resolute in her response hanging only on the fact that the license was incorrect. Her demand is that you let her out of the contract, but not for the full amount.

Please let me know how you'd like to respond and what counter you'd like to offer.

Talk tomorrow,

William

My feet go numb as the blood empties from them. All
I can hear is my family's laughter and joy that we're all
supposed to be experiencing during this happy time, yet my
fate hangs in the balance in my response. It appears Ms.
Broussard is not going to do this the easy way. I should've
assumed that when she went so far to file criminal charges,
normal people don't do that. Our society is changing to that
full of people anxiously waiting to become victims who
overreact to everything. It's not just the young ones. That's
what's most surprising.

My mom must have picked up on my stress because she
heads my way. She's probably been keeping her eye on me
all night, especially after Aunt Carolyn stopped me.

"What happened?" she asks as she sits in the chair next
to me.

"My attorney emailed. Ms. Broussard wouldn't drop the
charges or pay me the money she owes," I say solemnly.

"This woman! What does William say you should do?"
she asks incredulously. I'm not sure why I don't react the
way she does, I'm so beat down I feel defeated, and the battle hasn't even begun.

"All he asked was what I wanted to counter with. I thought he would counsel me on what to do, I just want a set of instructions on how I'm supposed to handle all this. I never knew something like this could happen, so how do I know what the right thing to do is? When do I fight, and when do I give in? Technically, in the eyes of the law, I was wrong, but gosh, the law says, 'Knowingly engages.' We didn't 'knowingly engage,' we're not frauds. We didn't set out to defraud anyone, and Ms. Broussard knows it. She's using this to her full advantage. How can they file charges if we didn't even know the license was wrong? I wish they would've talked to us, so we could've straightened this out." I'm breathless and feel my anxiety soar nearly out of control.

Momma suggests we go outside to get some air, and I relent.

On the patio, we talk about what my response should be. I know I need to call Allie and talk with her about what we should do. I forwarded her the email and said we'd talk tomorrow. My brain hurts too much tonight to make any sound decisions.

My phone wakes me the next morning. I must've been exhausted because I didn't intend to sleep this long. It's a text from our secretary saying to call her immediately.

"Hey Becca, is everything okay?" trying my best not to sound like I've been asleep.

"How can you be on vacation while Allie sits in jail?"

"What? What are you talking about?" I sit straight up in bed, but my brain is so foggy I can't comprehend what she's saying.

"Allie's mom called the office and said she's been arrested. She has a cousin who works at the Plaquemines Parish Sheriff's office that is helping her get out on bond," Becca says frantically, "Wait, I don't understand. Ms. Broussard filed the warrant against me, not her," I say, trying to put the pieces together in my head. I own majority of the company, and she didn't sign the contract.

"I don't know either, Audrey, but you have to help her."

"How do I get ahold of her? I can drive back in, but then I get arrested, and then where will we be?"

I hear my phone beep. Filled with relief, I see Allie's number.

"Allie's calling me, let me call you back," I can't say it quick enough, and I don't wait on Becca to respond as I click over to Allie.

"Allie?!" I almost scream.

"Hey," she sounds defeated and tired.

"What the heck happened?"

"I was at home this morning when a Plaquemines sheriff knocked on my door. He showed me my picture and asked me to identify myself. Then he showed me your picture and asked me to identify you. They were really nice, didn't even cuff me. I had Charles follow us up there to bail me out, walked in and out."

"Who's Charles?" I'm trying to catch all this information, but I can't keep up.

"My mom's cousin. He's a bail bondsman in Plaquemines Parish. My bail was $12,000, Audrey. The warrant was out of Jefferson Parish."

"Chad," we both say simultaneously. Dread rises in my chest.

"That means there're two warrants out for me in two separate parishes. How could he have known? Ms. Broussard must've gotten his contact information somehow and told him what to file. There's no way lightning strikes twice in this situation."

"I don't think you should come home," she says, and I'm filled with guilt.

"What do I do, Allie? Now we have to settle with *two* clients?"

"Let William know what's going on. I'm headed back

home now. I'm sorry this happened," her voice trails off. The guilt is obviously plaguing her too.

"*I'm* sorry. I can't believe they arrested you. How could we have known something like this could happen? We're not criminals. We're interior designers! Let me call William. I'll let you know what he says."

"Okay, talk to you soon."

William's secretary tells me he'll call me back once he gets out of depositions this morning. Meanwhile, I get dressed and head out to find my mom. She and my stepdad must've gotten up early. I'm rooming with them because I haven't had a paycheck since starting Magnolia Maison and have been living off my savings. We haven't even finished a project yet; who knows if we'll see the other end of this. We didn't budget for this amount of attorney fees or bail.

Finally, I find my mom and stepdad having brunch in the resort restaurant. My stepdad orders an omelet and orange juice for me before I can sit down. He takes such good care of my mom and me. I fill them in on all that's happened with Allie this morning. Overall, I think they're nervous for me. The wedding is tonight. They've booked the room for at least two more days, and I become more apprehensive that this will be settled in that amount of time.

"We can stay a couple more days, just need to make another reservation with the resort. Your mom and I have the time. At least while we wait and make sure the settlements are in place before you head back." My stepdad would sacrifice everything for me. He loves me like I'm his own, he never had kids and considers me his daughter. I've always loved that when he introduces me, it's as his "daughter" not his "stepdaughter."

"Hopefully, we can reach an agreement on the settlements and have the charges dropped soon. I'm not sure how much more of this I can take. Did I tell y'all that these were felonies? You can be charged with a felony for having the wrong license. Tell me that's not messed up."

We sit in silence for a moment. The thought of being charged with two felonies in two separate parishes overwhelms me. I'm not sure how they're handling it. I stare at the white linen tablecloth, not sure where to begin on these settlements. What is fair for us to accept from Ms. Broussard and now Chad that won't leave us bankrupt? At least we have some future projects that will hold us over until we can get this sorted out.

A few hours later, William calls me.

"Hey Audrey, it sounds like things aren't getting better, huh?"

I let out a huge breath, "I can't comprehend what's happening, William. Tell me there is something we can do. How can we fight this?"

"Unfortunately, there's not a lot we *can* do right now.

The hardest part of all of this is that they got you on a technicality. The law is black and white, and since you were operating without the proper license according to the law, then they can bring these charges against you."

"That wasn't what I wanted to hear," I trail off.

"I know. Listen, now we need to reach out to Mr. Ewing's attorney. Have you thought about what you're going to offer Ms. Broussard to settle?"

"They have me up against the wall. What is that called when someone takes advantage of a situation in exchange for something they want?"

"Extortion."

"Yes! How is it that what she's doing is legal? She owes *me* money for work that has already been completed. She just beat me to the punch. Or beat me with a punch. Terrible time for puns, I know."

"It's because of the license, Audrey," he gently reminds me.

I didn't really want him to answer my rhetorical question, hearing it makes it worse. I guess ignorance of the law really isn't an excuse.

Switching to business mode, I reply, "Let's see, I've done $80,000 worth of work on this project for her, to which she's only paid me $22,000. The basic math would be the $58,000, which she's not willing to pay, right? How am I supposed to respond?"

"That has to be your decision but come back with a number that you won't lose any money on the job."

I half-laugh, "I've already lost money if I accept less than $58,000. She's going to get this settlement as low as she wants because she has this arrest warrant hanging over my head. Then she gets all my work for free."

"Why don't you take some more time to think it over, and let's talk about Mr. Chad Ewing. Give me the backstory there."

"Where do I begin? I'm still shocked that he would do something like this. My contract says my clients are not supposed to talk to each other. Ms. Broussard must've coached Chad."

"We'll get to that in a minute. What kind of work are you doing for Mr. Ewing?" he says, trying to keep me on track.

"I went to high school with his son, so we've known each other for a while. He and his wife were going to re-model their house and went to my old firm looking for me, so I could do the work. My previous boss told Mr. and Mrs. Ewing I left to start my own company, so he called me and wanted to use me as his interior designer. Since he's a family friend, I bid the job at cost, so he wouldn't have to come out-of-pocket anything extra. Obviously, I will never do that again."

"Wait," he interrupts me, "you were doing his remodel *at cost*? You're saying there's no profit built into the project?"

"Yes, that's exactly what I'm saying. Anyway, I directed him to Tom Colliers at Liberty Bank in New Orleans, who I'm doing business with for some of our upcoming projects. He was approved for the loan, and we signed our contract back in February of this year."

"How much do you have into the project already?"

"We just got the last check from the bank and were scheduled to wrap up in a month or so. I'm not sure what he wants as a settlement."

"I'll reach out to his attorney, and we'll see what he says. I'll forward the response to you, and we'll go from there, okay?"

"Okay, thanks, William. Oh, there's one more thing. Chad's a lieutenant with the New Orleans Police Department."

7

A few hours before Mia's wedding, I decide to sit by the waterfront and gather my thoughts. Life seems simpler when it's quiet. Momentarily I abandon my fears and sit in God's presence. It is now an art to sit quietly without a phone, conversation, a book. Distraction. So much distraction. He's in the quiet when there are no distractions. It feels like I've added a new devotional for every time I've received bad news in the past few weeks. Suffice it to say I'm up to eight different devotionals. Sometimes sitting and listening for God's voice can be the answer.

A young girl catches my eye as she's walking along the bank. I've always loved watching people. Sometimes I create stories for them as I watch them in their busyness. Probably explains why my undergrad is Psychology. This young girl appears to be alone, which I find immediately odd because she's no younger than two years old. She swings her soft arms as she walks by me, not looking at me. Not even seeing me. At first, I'm taken by her beauty. Her brown hair falls in soft curls, and her skin has been tanned by the sun. She reminds me of my niece. I look around, waiting on her parents to follow behind her, but I don't see anyone. She keeps walking with a determined step, and I become more worried that she is walking so close to the water and no adult is around. I watch as she continues walking farther away from me.

"Go to her," I hear softly.

I look around and see no one. I turn my head back around to the little girl, and she is getting farther and farther away. Laying my notebook down, I jog toward her.

"Hey, sweetie," I half yell as I run to catch up to her.

Finally, I reach her and ask where her parents are.

"Papa," she faintly says.

"Yes, sweetheart, are you looking for your papa?"

"Papa," she says again. Her hazel eyes stare into mine. I'm not sure what to do. I keep looking around, waiting on someone to rush up and claim her. No one.

"How old are you, sweetie?"

She stares at me.

A couple walks past us, and I ask them desperately, "Have you seen this little girl around here? Or anyone she was with? I think she might be lost."

"Oh my goodness," says the woman.

"No, we haven't seen her," the husband says.

"Well, she was walking this way," I point along the bank in the direction she's walking. "Maybe she's going back to where she came from? But I'd hate to walk with her and be walking away from where she came from." The little girl reaches for my hand, and I gladly take it, hoping to offer any sort of comfort I can to her.

"We should probably call 911 and report her missing," the husband says as he scans the horizon for help.

"Should we take her to the help desk in the lobby? Surely, she and her family are staying here," I add.

We make our way to the lobby, and we're greeted halfway by a man wearing a resort uniform, complete with a walkie-talkie.

"Is that Lilly?" he shouts in our direction and points to the little girl holding my hand.

"I'm not sure, she is only saying, 'Papa.' Is she missing because I found her walking along the bank?"

"Yep, I bet that's her. Hey there," he says to Lilly as he reaches us. He squats, trying to talk to her, but she hides her face in my leg and grips my hand even tighter. I don't let go and give her head a soft rub letting her know it's okay.

"Hey Lilly, do you want to go see your Momma? She's really worried about you," he tries again.

She doesn't respond and keeps her face in my leg.

"I don't mind walking her up to where her mom is. She's probably scared."

"Okay, I'll show you the way," he replies.

We walk a little more, and then I see a woman out of the corner of my eye running up to us.

"There you are! Your mom is worried about you!" she yells to Lilly as she holds a Styrofoam cup in one hand.

Lilly squeezes my hand. Although I've only met her, I want to protect her.

"Let's go see your Momma!" she says as she scoops her up and walks away before I can react. Thankfully the resort employee follows them. I'm not sure what else to do as I watch them walk up the hill. I thank the couple who stopped to help and say a silent prayer for Lilly on my walk back to my chair on the dock. What happened so quickly ended so abruptly too.

About fifteen minutes later, the resort employee came back to update me.

"The lady that came and got her was supposed to be watching her. Lilly walked for what must've been a quarter of a mile before she noticed she was gone."

My heart sinks.

"Where was her mom?" I ask.

"She was eating lunch and having a margarita or two in the resort restaurant."

My stomach turns. "She was asking for her papa. Did they get her to him?"

"Yeah, he met us in the lobby to get her."

"I don't understand. I realize that that can happen to anyone, but the whole situation leaves me unnerved."

"You'd be surprised how many missing reports we get on children, especially during the summer," he finishes.

"That's awful."

Neither of us knowing what else to say, we stay silent for a moment. He's then called to some other need, like towels or an ice machine on the fritz, that beckons him from his walkie-talkie.

"Thanks for your help. That could've ended so differently," he says before he leaves.

His final statement bounces around in my brain. It could have ended differently, but God told me to go to her. God is always in the whisper. The tugging at your heart to do the right thing, to give of yourself. Little did I know the tugging on my heart would continue throughout my own trials. Obedience doesn't come naturally. We want to kick and scream, letting our emotions take the wheel. Grace and obedience are hard-fought but worth the battle win.

I don't receive any emails from William for the next two days. Part of me realizes that each day that passes is another day that we haven't reached an agreement, and the arrest warrants are still active.

Finally, on Wednesday afternoon, my email dings a message titled "Ewing & Broussard Settlements."

Audrey,

Chad Ewing wants you to give him back the final draw and to terminate the contract with Magnolia Maison.

I've also heard again from Ms. Broussard's attorney stating that Ms. Broussard will only give $35,000 in order to drop the charges against you.

Let me know what you think. Hope you're doing okay.

William

I immediately call Allie. She picks up after what feels like an eternity.

"Hey, Audrey, what's going on?"

"I just forwarded you William's email about Chad and

Ms. Broussard's settlement request. He wants us to return the money from his final draw, and Ms. Broussard won't give us any more than $35,000."

I hear her suck in a breath. "What? How did she arrive at that number? There's $35,000 in furniture alone!"

"I know," I trail off. "We have to settle with these people, I don't want to risk going to court because we don't know what kind of people we're dealing with at this point. According to Sandy Colefield at the Board, the law is black and white."

"But we weren't practicing without a license, it was *just* the wrong one. That has to be a technicality. The line is too fine to split hairs on this one. We never did anything intentionally; can't they see that? No one has given us the opportunity to tell them what happened. We've been deemed guilty until proven innocent," she finally finishes and sounds defeated.

"Oh, I know they see that. But right now, it's not about whether they know we weren't trying to 'defraud' anyone. They're trying to take full advantage of our mistake. The problem is that they're getting into a herd mentality, and they have a common enemy—us. We live in a new society where everyone is a victim, and if they can spin it for their benefit, they will."

"They would go so far to throw us in jail? And make us lose all this money for bail?" Allie says breathlessly.

"I'm slowly figuring out that, yes, that is exactly how far they will go. We are behind the eight ball at this point, and we have to play catch up by digging ourselves out of this hole. Right now, they've played all their cards, and we need to determine how to get out of this without seeking vengeance. We have to turn the other cheek, right our wrongs, and move on."

"What? We're not going to fight this?"

"How can we, Allie? We don't have the funds to fight this civilly, and neither do they. You've already spent $12,000 to get out of one jail. And if we don't get this settled, I'll have to go to two. Did you know it is really expensive to hire a lawyer and file a civil lawsuit, let alone the time it takes to reach an agreement that way? On the other hand, it's free to file a criminal charge. Tell me now how you think they came to their solution. I've been doing a lot of research on cases like ours and the law in Louisiana. There is no wiggle room, and we're going to have to walk through this. I am going to email William back and tell him that we will return Chad's money if he drops the charges. And as far as Ms. Broussard is concerned, I'm going to have to get with our accountant to run the numbers and see how much we can afford to lose. I'm afraid we've already met the threshold for losing more than we can afford. I want to kick myself for making that deal with Chad. I never should've done the contract at cost."

Heading back to the room, I call our accountant to

crunch the numbers before responding to William.

"This is a big hit, Audrey," Lisa exhales as the sounds of her shuffling paper can be heard through the phone.

"I know, but I'm not sure how to get out of it since the stupid license was wrong. I never would've predicted this."

"Give me a few minutes, and I'll let you know how bad it is and how low of a settlement Magnolia Maison can offer."

"Thanks, Lisa."

While I wait for Lisa to send over the spreadsheet, the thought that I have to leave in two days sinks in, and the likelihood that we'll have these settled *is* virtually impossible. I have to come up with a plan just in case.

8

Good morning William,

After speaking with Allie and my accountant, we'd like to give the money back to Mr. Ewing as long as he drops the charges against us. In addition, we agree to terminate the contract with him and Mrs. Ewing.

However, we cannot accept Ms. Broussard's offer of $35,000. We would like to counter with $45,000 so Magnolia Maison doesn't go bankrupt. Regardless of the issue with the license, money has been spent on her home that we need returned in order to survive this.

Thank you,

Audrey.

"Sent," I say to my mom. We've packed our bags and determined it best that I go to my aunt and uncle's house in Jasper, Texas. I really thought we'd have all this settled before time to leave. I keep expecting miracles and peace, but I can't find either. My mom is nervous about me driving to Jasper, so I agree to call her frequently when she's not on the plane. I wish our time together wouldn't have been clouded by my grief. We prayed many times a day. When we both felt afraid, we prayed.

My nearly five-hour drive to Jasper was depressing. It rained the whole way, a reflection of how I felt inside. I found K-Love in every town I passed through. God was silent, and I didn't understand why. Those many hours I cried and drove with my eyes constantly on the rearview and odometer. Fear drove me to Jasper.

I stopped for gas in Carthage. While I waited at the pump, I decided to check Magnolia Maison's social media pages. So far, no bad press had gotten out, but that didn't abate any fears I had that it would, so I checked it frequently. We hadn't posted in a while because I didn't want to attract any undue attention. Still, nothing, my tension eased.

About thirty minutes later, I hear my Facebook Pages notification go off. Then it went off again. My phone must have dinged at least ten times before I could pull off the road to check it. All the blood left my body when I saw what someone had commented on one of our pictures, "Crooks." As I scrolled down, I realized they wrote it on every single picture we had. A modern-day version of graffiti plastered all over our page. I immediately unpublished the page because I couldn't delete the comments fast enough. A pictureless profile with the name "Donald Jay" was the culprit. I clicked on his name. He had no friends, no pictures, and no activity on his page. A fake profile and conveniently shared our president's name. Judging that it was on Facebook, I knew it was one of my older clienteles since they didn't take to Instagram. I doubted Ms. Broussard would do this, so it left Chad or Mr. Emerson. All roads led to Mr. Emerson since he's a big Trump supporter. He could've been more creative than that. Wasn't this a textbook definition of slander? Problem was that I couldn't prove it was Mr. Emerson, not easily anyway.

Mr. Emerson had been sending some unpleasant emails since I'd been out of town. Business had come to a stop, and I had to let him know Magnolia Maison was ordered to cease and desist. At first, I thought he was fine with it, now apparently not. He commented under one of Chad's comments. Hopefully, they're not connected now. What a mess this was turning into. Moving my thoughts back to the road, I prayed the rest of the way to Jasper and convinced myself I'd have this handled and under control once I could stop and think.

Finally, after an exhausting last leg of the trip, I pull into the gravel driveway of my aunt and uncle's place. It's dusk in Texas, the beautiful kind where the trees look black with the sun at their backs. Whether rising or setting, the sun is always more beautiful in Texas. My aunt comes to greet me before I'm out of the car. She wraps me in her arms and lets me cry for what feels like ages. She keeps whispering, "I know, I know."

We finally break apart as my uncle shouts from the porch, "Oh quit it an' get in here, I got banana puddin'."

My uncle Jimmy Wayne, everyone calls him J. W., can best be described as a good ol' country boy. He's in his sixties, has salt and pepper hair, and a round belly from my aunt's homemade cooking. You can tell he used to be a tall, handsome glass of water, but life has aged him, and now his humor replaces the hard edges that once were. He'll never let you forget how lean and fit he used to be. Their home is a modest burnt red color. When you walk in the door, the smell of bacon grease and burning firewood fills your nose. Small, ceramic cherub figurines line the wallpapered kitchen walls. It's always reminded me of my grandparent's house. I've never been able to tell if it's the smell of cooking food, the warmth of the wood-burning fireplace, or the laughter and playful arguments over a game of dominoes that makes this place so homey. Regardless, it's one place I'm glad to be because it's filled with love and family.

"What ya got yourself into now?" J. W. half-shouts. He's always been a loud talker. My Aunt Peggy always slaps him on the arm and reminds him that he's screaming. Hearing loss has nothing to do with it, he's just loud.

"Do ya at least have a good lawyer?" He keeps talking.

"Yes, J. W. He's trying to work it out."

"Well, ya gotta watch the lawyers. They're out to get your money and some work behind your back with those judges."

"I am. William is working really hard for us, and I have

no doubt he'll help us figure this whole thing out," I reply.

"You better. Don't say I didn't warn ya. Now, I got some banana puddin' I made this afternoon." When J. W. is done talking on a subject, everyone knows to drop it. He doesn't really know his way around the kitchen, but the one thing he knows how to make is banana pudding. And to be honest, it's always delicious. He takes the job very seriously. Aunt Peggy has to gather the ingredients and set him up at the end of the counter, where he bellies up and begins cutting bananas. He doesn't move the entire time, if he's forgotten an ingredient, he not so delicately yells for Aunt Peggy to "get it for him" in his southern drawl that usually starts with, "Git me." The feminists wouldn't get along very well with him, but Aunt Peggy does it because she loves him. Sometimes I think feminists believe women are stuck in the kitchen or stuck at home rearing babies and that they don't want to be there, but maybe that's exactly where they want to be. Maybe they don't think of themselves as trapped or that there is a better life for them. Maybe they're happy right where they are. My Aunt Peggy sure is, although as she's gotten older, she sometimes tires of her kids and husband needing her all the time.

Aunt Peggy and J. W. live in a small town where the junior suffixes reign supreme. No one knows whether it's that they're not inventive or they're really proud of their sons. Probably a mixture of both. J. W.'s son is a junior and lives right down the lane with his wife and three kids. Jasper

89

is a place where everyone already knows your business if you're on every First Baptist and Assembly of God prayer list. I've already been put on the lists because of my aunt's prayer warriors. In the past, I'd be offended or embarrassed. Now I welcome the prayers. They're always listed under "Unspoken Prayer Request," but those with cancer or health issues are brandished all over the page. This is the first time I've realized that although it's a huge mistake, it's one I won't get much support for and who has the time to sit around and listen to the whole story? They don't start meal trains for felons. Even those that are wrongfully charged because if they've charged you, they must've done an investigation. They wouldn't arrest you for no reason. They'd do their due diligence, or maybe not. Failure has a funny way of making you humble.

It's like I've stepped foot back into 1952. Life is simpler here, and I'm hoping to find the peace and settlements I'm searching for. Time and Microsoft Outlook will only tell.

A typical Friday evening at Aunt Peggy and J. W.'s house is already in motion when I arrive. Aunt Peggy's cooking fried deer meat, and her slew of grandchildren sit on the floor with their tablets. J. W. is in his brown recliner that points directly at the TV, which is on Wheel of Fortune. He never misses an episode, and it's usually accompanied by him either ridiculing the contestants or saying how "dang good" they are. My cousins and their wives are here. Anytime company comes, the whole family is present and ready to greet them. Aunt Peggy loves a house full of family.

I go through the routine of explaining what happened and why I'm there, answering all their questions of why I didn't do this or that I *should* do this or that. Most of them encourage me to go after these people with all I have. I'm reminded of when I broke my arm as an elementary school kid and had to explain and re-explain how I broke my arm, what I felt, what I did, what others did, what I shouldn't have done. They can't sign my cast this time, though. The injury is too great and invisible.

"If it were me, I'd do criminal charges against all of 'em," my cousin Junior says. He's Aunt Peggy and J. W.'s eldest son and has all the advice for me. He means well, but it's exhausting trying to tell him why it's not right to play tit-for-tat.

"Well, I'd definitely go after that Sandy Colefield lady at the Board. She started this whole thing it sounds like," Junior continues.

"I'm not sure how I can, William is concerned that if I go after the Board, then I won't have their support in the future."

"You don't have it now!" J. W. pipes in. I didn't realize he'd been listening.

"I'm tellin' ya, these people don't care who ya are or that ya made a mistake. They don't care that you're young or whether you meant to or not. They're heartless. You're in business, and they see ya as a business, not a person. They're makin' an example outta ya."

I'm taken aback by his emphatic speech. J. W. is not a man who minces words, but I know he has a good heart. His passion is because he's upset they've come after me. I've always been his favorite niece. Part of me worried to come here since I have arrest warrants in another state. But Aunt Peggy didn't give it a second thought, she and J. W. wanted to protect me while I worked it out. They don't want me to face the horrible experience of going to jail.

After dinner, Aunt Peggy sets the kids up in the living room watching a movie, so the adults can have the kitchen table for dominoes. Momentarily I've forgotten why I'm here and begin to relax after the fourth game of Shoot the Moon. We belly laugh and rib each other as shouts of "he's shootin' the moon!" and "y'all cheated" surround the table. Everyone is a sore loser and sore winner. About midnight, the kids are all sound asleep on the floor, and we head to bed.

9

The smell of rich, strong coffee wakes me. J. W. gets up at 4:00 every morning, weekend or not. This explains why he always falls asleep in his chair during the day. I decide to get up and check my email. I've learned to silence any notifications after 9:00 p.m. since Mr. Emerson has been flooding my inbox with emails that range from awful accusations to pleas of desperation to finish his project. I don't know how else to explain to him that if I continue work on his project, I will get into real trouble and potentially lose Magnolia Maison altogether. Part of me wonders whether he's trying to bait me into doing work on the project. I'm jaded and assume no one has good intentions anymore.

Much as I suspected, he's sent four emails staggered every fifteen minutes. The first is titled "Please help," and the last is "You're going to hell." They always spiral out of control if I don't answer him immediately. But I've learned even if I do answer, his tactic is to get me on the phone and record me—this from a Christian man. What concerns me most is the way his demeanor has changed in the last week. He and his wife considered me family and were so proud that they were one of my first clients. Now, it's like I don't know the man, and he suspects I'm trying to hurt him intentionally. I fear that Chad has gotten in his ear.

Curiosity gets the best of me, and I open the last email.

"You're going to hell for what you've done. You cannot hide from me because I will find you."

My anxiety soars. What is going on with these people? They truly think that I started this whole thing to defraud them. It's being shed in the wrong light, and no one is listening or believing me. Mr. Emerson's project is 90 percent complete. Why would I do that much work if I was defrauding them? There would be no work done on any of their projects. A thought tickles the back of my brain. He said that I can't hide. How does he know I'm hiding? The only thing I told him was that for the time being, we had to stop work on his project until we received our correct license. Chad has gotten to him. Fear grips my heart. Will he file a criminal charge as well? I immediately start to pray for protection and peace. I know I can't handle this emotionally on my own.

I send out the bat signal to my elementary school friends. We only send this if one of us is in a desperate situation. At the moment, I'm too embarrassed to say what happened. Just that I'm in dire need of their prayers involving my company, and it's too much to put into a text. My phone rings, it's one of my best friends, Laura. I've known her since we were in 2nd grade. She lives in the Houston area now, so we don't get to see each other except around the holidays.

"Hey Audrey, is everything okay? Your text worried me."

"Oh gosh, Laura, I don't know anymore. To be honest, I'm scared. This mess is bigger than I ever imagined it could get."

"What's going on?"

Again, I retell the story of what happened, detailing what Mr. Emerson sent and the active arrest warrants. I leave nothing out. This is my first test of telling someone outside of my family and work. Her reaction is a relief.

I hear her inhale sharply, "That is unbelievable!"

"You're telling me. I feel like I'm living someone else's life. I never imagined something like this could happen to me. And to be honest, I'm terrified."

"I bet so. Listen, I feel led to pray over you right now."

She prays, and I sob silently, thankful that she understands how I feel. Her prayer is so genuine and heartfelt I truly feel understood and not alone. When she's done, she offers to come visit me, but for now, I'm okay and don't want to take her away from her family. We say goodbye, and she promises that she'll check in on me and to reach out to her anytime. I thank her and tell her how much I love and appreciate her support. Our friendship grew exponentially in that phone call. She took the time to make sure I was okay.

Aunt Peggy must've heard me because she lightly knocks on the wooden door.

"Come in," I say quietly, trying to dry my eyes.

"Mornin'," she says, handing me a cup of coffee.

"Thanks, Aunt Peggy."

"You want some bacon and eggs?" Aunt Peggy knows that food can always help heal.

"Sure, what can I do to help? I don't want to be a burden for you."

"Oh sweetheart, you're not a burden. I enjoy havin' you here." She pauses a moment before continuing, "I heard you on the phone. Is everything okay?"

"Yes, ma'am, I was talking to my friend Laura. She prayed over me after I read a scathing email from one of my clients."

"I don't know how you do it, Audrey," she sympathetically sighs. "And I don't know why they're doing this either."

"One moment at a time. Sometimes I can't see anything in front of me except this struggle. I keep praying that this will be over soon, but I don't see a way out. They don't just drop charges, or do they?"

"That I don't know. Here's what I do know without a

doubt: God is in control of this situation. We may not understand it or why God allows things like this to happen to sweet people like you, but we have to trust and have faith that He is protecting you even in the midst of your storm. Keep your chin up and continue seeking His direction for your life. He ordains every step you take and longs for your happiness in Him. It will all work itself out."

She gives my leg a pat, tells me to get dressed and heads out the door.

After everyone eats breakfast, the kids head outside to play, and the men go to the shop to meddle with tools. J. W. and Aunt Peggy live on an acre of beautiful land surrounded by pastures that are freckled with horses and cows. Sunset is my favorite here when the crickets chirp their goodnight lullabies, and you can see every star in the sky. This place is magical in this small town in Texas. The city could never compare to this secret country oasis.

I sit by the campfire Aunt Peggy made and read my Bible. Most people would think it odd to have a campfire during the day, but I think this is Aunt Peggy's greatest kept secret. The smell of the rich pine burning in the air is nature in a bottle that no candle or essential oil could ever compare.

A storm is set to blow in later, so I take in nature while I can. There's something beautiful about sitting outside and just existing. Breathing in the fresh air and letting the sun kiss your cheeks. You can be made whole by sitting outside with the sun at your face and your feet in the grass.

The weekend goes by without any emails from Mr. Emerson or William. I count these lucky days because I need a break from my anxiety and thoughts.

Monday morning doesn't disappoint. Right at 8 a.m., Mr. Emerson starts calling me. We have the same conversation we've had since we discovered our license was wrong. Magnolia Maison is ordered to cease and desist. All he wants is his project complete, I explain I can't until the Board gives us a new one. Same conversation, different day, and he still either doesn't understand or refuses to accept my answer. I keep to the script, though, so I don't get myself into even more trouble. I listen to him rant and rave and attempt to appease him that work should begin back soon and that I will keep him apprised as soon as I know something new. That temporarily abates him.

Mid-morning, I receive a text from my previous boss asking me to give her a call when I'm available. Good news or bad news? I can't even tell anymore, but *I'm* assuming the worst. I call her right away.

"Hey Audrey, that was quick. I haven't heard from you in a while, how are things?" she asks genuinely.

"Well, I'm not sure how to quickly describe what I've had to deal with, but first, I could ask if you've heard anything about what's going on."

She lets out a slow exhale, "Yes, Chad called me on Friday."

My mind reels as she says this. "What? What for?"

"Well, I hope none of what he's told me is true."

"What exactly *did* he tell you?" I frantically ask.

Another exhale, "To start, he's saying that you stole the job from me and that my company should sue you."

"Oh my gosh, Lynn! I…" I can hardly contain my anger.

"Listen," she interrupts me, "before you start, let me say this: I don't believe that. I knew you were working with Chad and that it was his idea to go with your company. That's not what I'm concerned about. He said that you defrauded him, something about your license and that they're trying to arrest you."

"This is almost unbelievable," I sit there for a moment, trying to gather my thoughts and control my rage.

"Allie had the wrong license, still an interior design one, but not the correct one. We didn't defraud anyone. It was a complete misunderstanding that we tried to fix immediately."

"He also said that you're about to lose your house," she says quietly.

At this, I'm at a loss for words.

She waits for me to process what she's said, then I finally reply, "How would he know that?"

"I'm not sure, Audrey, but he's made several other accusations that sound pretty serious."

"Like what?"

"He's saying you committed bank fraud."

A knot develops in the pit of my stomach. This is the final straw, and I begin to cry. It feels like I cry for ages, but this is the first time I've truly understood the severity of my situation, and it hits me like a ton of bricks.

"I don't even know what bank fraud is."

"I'm not sure either," is all she says. "I'm worried about you."

"I need to reassess and figure out what is going on. Do you mind if I call you later?" I ask.

"Absolutely. Please update me and let me know if you need anything," she replies sincerely.

"Thanks, Lynn, for letting me know. Most people would've assumed the worst, especially when a police officer is making these accusations."

"I know, it threw me off at first, but I know you and that you wouldn't do anything he was saying. It just sounded like you were in one heck of a pickle."

"Thanks again. I'll call you later."

"One last thing, have you thought about contacting your state representative? They could probably help with the issues at the Board."

"I will look it up, I need to figure this bank fraud thing out first."

My fingers fly to the internet app, and I hastily begin typing "what is bank fraud?" into the search bar on my phone. What I read isn't remotely related to our situation. That sounds federal, and I decide to call Charles, Allie's bail bondsman, to ask him what the charges are against me.

"Hi there, Ms. Tribb. Okay, here's what I've learned from Jefferson and St. Tammany parishes. 'Interior Design Fraud' in both parishes. Bond in Jefferson is $40,000, and St. Tammany is $12,000," he finishes.

"Okay, thank you. Just to update you, we're currently trying to settle out of court with both clients in these parishes. Once they drop the charges, the warrants won't be active anymore, right?"

"Um, I've never heard of them recalling an arrest warrant. Not even one in ten, but I've never personally seen it happen. Once that arrest warrant is issued, they're going to arrest you, plain and simple."

"Even if we settle before then?" I ask, not sure I want to hear his answer.

"Well, there is a slim possibility, but these are felony charges. Let me explain the process to you. Your clients met with a detective who determined that you indeed broke the law. The detective completes an investigation and takes the information to the parish District Attorney who then decides whether they want to pursue you. The District Attorney then takes the same information to the judge who decides whether an arrest warrant should be issued."

"But no one has talked to me. There was no investigation done, to begin with!" I don't feel like I'm breathing. No one is listening to me.

"I'm sorry that you guys are in this position. Save my phone number, give it to your family members, and if you get arrested, let me know, and we'll get you out," Charles finishes. He sounds pleasant but overworked and probably has conversations like this every day.

"I appreciate your time."

When we hang up, I'm not sure how to breathe. I am relieved that he didn't mention bank fraud. What was Chad talking about?

Dear God, I ask for Your protection. Lord, I'm not sure why all this is happening. I felt so strongly that this is what You wanted me to do. I prayed and heard You so clearly last year. You opened doors that only You could open. Thank You for Your protection so far and never leaving me. I am afraid God, I'm not sure where this is headed, but I trust You completely. Please give me peace that passes all understanding, and only You can provide. In Your precious name, amen.

10

Audrey,

Mr. Ewing has accepted your settlement offer. He will drop the charges if you return his last draw.

Ms. Broussard does not accept your offer and stands by her original offer of $35,000. They are prepared to move to the second stage of discovery for evidence and then proceed to court.

My advice is to settle with Ms. Broussard. The license will hurt you if we go to court, and I'm afraid you won't get anything back. On top of that, civil litigation is very costly. I want you to make an informed decision and get back with me.

William

I forward the email to Allie and ask what she thinks we should do. In the meantime, I begin my email to my state representative. Another quick internet search determined Calvin Maxwell's office was who I needed to contact.

The final draft was six paragraphs long and took three hours to write. I told him everything, that no one has contacted me, the license error, the Interior Design Board, and their investigator Sandy Colefield mishandled the situation. I also let him know that William was my attorney to let him know that I wasn't seeking legal advice. Maybe one of his temps would read it, and they'd see that we needed help.

Later that afternoon, Allie called to talk about Ms. Broussard.

"I think we should accept her offer and get her out of our hair. From what William says, going to court could cost us more money," I tell her.

The sound of her annoyance comes through, "So what she's done is filed criminal charges against us knowing that we'd be desperate to settle. Then offers a laughable amount because she knows she can't get away with paying us nothing."

"Overall, yes," I sigh.

"Fine," she quips through clenched teeth.

"I've reached out to our state representative Calvin Maxwell, maybe we can turn this thing around with his help. It all started at the Board."

"Maybe," she replies.

I know her irritation has nothing to do with me because I feel the same way. My anger, though, has subsided into fear. Ms. Broussard's tactic worked. She's terrified me into doing whatever she demands.

The days begin to blend into each other—coffee, email, phone calls, dinner, dishes, Wheel of Fortune, repeat. I still haven't heard from Calvin Maxwell's office after two days, so I decide to call.

"State Representative Calvin Maxwell's office," answers a chipper woman.

"Morning, this is Audrey Tribb with Magnolia Maison. I emailed Mr. Maxwell two days ago. I wondered whether he had an opportunity to read it and offer any kind of advice."

"Oh, hi there, Ms. Tribb. Thank you for calling. Yes, I mentioned the email to him. He said he'd read it on his flight to his son's wedding this weekend."

For the moment, I'm hopeful, "Great! I'm here to answer any questions if he has them. I just want him to understand the seriousness of these accusations and that no one is listening to us. We need help," I try not to sound desperate but urgent.

"He may not respond until next week when he gets back, but I will make sure he knows you've called," she says.

"Thank you." Finally, I feel like we're being heard.

The weekend goes by slowly. Aunt Peggy and I visit estate sales and the local farmer's market. It's nice to get out and know that no one knows me here. I don't feel afraid, but there is a small amount of fear that worries whether the police will pull up and arrest me in public. The thought fills me with shame. I know the truth, and I must cling to that, not what these people are accusing me of.

The weather is crisp as the leaves change their skin to the warmer reds, yellows, and oranges of fall. Death never was so beautiful. As we pass by the jars of jellies and pickles, my head swims with the thought of a state representative championing us and being our voice. My mood is instantly lifted. Maybe we'll have a storybook ending after all.

Aunt Peggy buys two boxes of fresh vegetables and a few jars of jelly she plans to use for Thanksgiving dinner. She loves to host and cook, so Thanksgiving is her favorite holiday. I was hoping to be home by Thanksgiving, but as the days drag on, I'm not sure of anything anymore. But I've already been in Texas two weeks, and settlements have just now been agreed on.

I sent William an email confirming that we'd settle with Ms. Broussard for the amount she demanded. We needed to get this thing behind us and back to work. The board is supposed to have a hearing next week. They'll have a segment where they will approve or deny new license applications. Magnolia Maison's application is supposed to be determined then. Hopefully, all this can be settled next week, and we can move on from this. I don't have a plan if we're denied.

On Sunday, I get a text message from a number I don't recognize, "Ms. Tribb, this is Jackie's mom. Can we speak sometime today?"

Oh, no, I think. Not again. Jackie was referred to me by Ms. Broussard months ago and also lives in St. Tammany Parish. We haven't started her project yet but have signed a contract. Jackie is my age and wanted me to help with her first home.

I respond back, "Hi there! I'd love to chat with you today. What time is good for you?"

She responds immediately, "I am free after I get out of church around 1:00."

"Great! I will call you then." Dread takes root in my chest, again. I pray that this doesn't end the same way the others have. Relieved she's not available right now. I begin to develop a game plan for how I'm going to handle this conversation.

At first, I find it odd that Jackie's mom would reach out to me. However, we do live in the south, where mothers meddle and fiercely protect their young. This thought makes me even warier, and my chest begins to ache. I decide to take an anxiety pill that hides in my purse. I try to only use them for occasions like these. It seems I'm reaching for them more often nowadays.

Instead of parking myself in front of the TV with everyone else, I sit in my room and read my Bible. My eyes keep on the clock. I have two hours. I'm awoken by loud arguing in the living room. Panic sets in as I reach for my phone to see what time it is, 12:45. Relief floods me as my attention turns to the raised voices.

"I'm going to move my stand over there by the gate," Junior says.

"Nah, that's a terrible place, you'd get too much traffic from the road, deer'll never come by there," J. W. replies.

"That's not what Wade said. He saw four deer over there Friday."

"No, he didn't, he's just tryin' to get you to move out of your honey hole!" J. W. shouts at him.

The walls are paper thin. What sounded like shouting was just them talking. I've realized that in my time here. They sound like they're arguing because they are trying to yell over the TV, but most of the time are sitting only three feet from each other. Only fifteen minutes until I need to call Jackie's mom. I rehearse in my mind what I'm going to say. A thought crosses my mind that I need to go somewhere quiet to talk with her. I grab my phone and head outside.

She answers on the second ring.

"Hi Ms. Tribb, thanks for calling me," she says sweetly.

"Anytime. I didn't catch your name," I say, trying not to sound awkward.

"Sonja."

"Ms. Sonja, what can I help with?"

She takes a breath, "Ms. Broussard told me what was going on with these charges she's got against you."

I inhale sharply, trying to remain calm, "Yes, ma'am, it's awful. We had no idea the license was wrong, but we've already put our application in for the right one," I quickly add.

"A detective came by our house last week. Ms. Broussard was with him. It felt like they were trying to force us to press charges against you. Said it would make their case stronger. Jackie wouldn't have it. Now, I'm a Christian woman, and I don't think anyone should go to jail over something like this." I try to hold back my tears and elation while I say a silent prayer of thanks.

"Ms. Sonja, that gives me so much relief and hope in humanity. I was beginning to wonder if I was as bad as they're making me out to be."

"Sweetheart, I don't know you yet, but my Jackie speaks highly of you. What they're doing to you is wrong, and I told them that. I made them leave my house and told them we were not pressing charges."

"I really don't think I can express how thankful I am that someone can see what really happened, none of this was on purpose, and I wish it never happened. We've been given a cease and desist, so we won't be able to start work on Jackie's project."

"That's another thing I wanted to talk with you about. She has decided not to go forward with re-designing her new home for now. I'm sorry, but she'd like her deposit back and to be let out of the contract," she finishes quietly.

"I appreciate your honesty. I can't blame her for not wanting to continue considering all that's happened. Sometimes I wonder whether I do."

"Please don't let them do that to you. Keep fighting and find your way out of this mess and come back stronger than ever before. Do it for you, not for them, and certainly not for revenge. The Lord will make it right. He knows your heart."

Her sincere advice catches me off guard. This is better than I thought it would be. We still lost another client. Under the circumstances, I will consider it a win, for now, no new arrest warrants.

"Please keep me updated on what's going on with you. I will pray for you and for this all to clear up in your favor."

Having Ms. Sonja and Jackie's support reignites my

energy, and I begin to believe the truth will eventually come out how these people have tried to come after me maliciously. It gives me hope.

11

Disappointingly by Wednesday, I haven't heard from State Representative Calvin Maxwell's office. On Monday afternoon, I received a phone call from a Board investigator, Bryant Murray, out of Jefferson Parish. He is investigating since Chad filed a complaint at the board. Kind and soft-spoken, he asked general questions about Allie's license, the contracts we've developed, and how much we have completed on Chad's project. These questions were more like an investigation, contrarily from the "investigation" Sandy Colefield failed to do. She ran with what little information she had, took Ms. Broussard's lies, and guided her with her detective friend to file criminal charges.

"Okay, I will include all of this information in my notes that will go to the Board for review. I think that's all I need. Do you have any questions, Ms. Tribb?"

"Actually, yes, sir, I do. What is the likelihood that we will get our license?" I ask.

"As long as you've completed the application and provide everything they ask, I'm sure it won't be a big deal for you to get it. I'm recommending they give it to you in my report. I can tell by the way you describe what happened that it wasn't on purpose. This could've happened to anyone."

"Thank you so much, Mr. Murray. I can't tell you how much that means to me. Another investigator, Sandy Colefield, from St. Tammany Parish, has helped one of our other clients file criminal charges against us. I never thought they could do something like that, arrest someone for a license issue. I get not having a license and knowingly working as an interior designer, but we had the wrong type of interior design license. In my opinion, that's a misinterpretation of the law and shouldn't be a felony. Anyway, I know you don't make those decisions. I'm just very frustrated by this whole thing."

"Oh wow, yeah, I'm just doing my investigation. Unfortunately, you're right, I don't make decisions for the Board."

"Yes, sir, I understand that. Thanks again for your time, and please let me know if you have any more questions."

"Sure thing, good luck to you," he finishes.

I'm overjoyed. It appears there's a light at the end of this tunnel, and people are listening after all.

After our conversation, I check our application status on the Board's website. Nothing has changed since I looked last night. All the checkboxes are marked. Our application is complete and ready to be presented at this month's Board meeting. Now we wait for a decision.

Out of curiosity, I spend some time looking around at

the Board's website from the client's perspective. All over the home page is how to file a complaint. In fact, you can do it from the comfort of your own home. The only thing you have to have is the name of the company, its address, and contact information of the owner. This is way too easy, yet there is zero support on what to do as an interior designer who's been accused of something so ludicrous. The thought keeps creeping up in the back of my mind that there must be more people this has happened to, and I'm sickened by it. What I learned from the Compliance Director, Robert Thompson, all those weeks ago, was that they really only hand out fines for companies who have a licensing issue. He also said that they want me to have my license. The more mistakes I make, the more money they make. They don't want me to go to jail because they can't make any money off me. It will be interesting to see if that is how this all plays out, hunger and greed for money.

The Board is set to have their monthly meeting on Friday in Baton Rouge to determine if we get our license. For the time being, I try to keep a handle on the company's business, mainly keeping Mr. Emerson appeased, so it doesn't get much worse. I'm hopeful but also wary of what the decision will be. I spend most of my waking hours trying to figure out what we're going to do if we don't get the license. Can we reapply? Do I switch careers entirely or go back to work for Lynn? Deep down in my heart, I know God is in control of all this; however, most days, my fears get the best of me. I worry and worry.

The day before the Board is set to meet, a St. Charles Parish number calls me. The only person I know there is Mr. and Mrs. Emerson. I answer, thinking it's Mr. Emerson on his landline.

"This is Audrey Tribb," I answer in case it's someone else.

"Ms. Tribb, this is Victor Barton, an investigator for the Interior Design Board for St. Charles Parish." He sounds older, and his voice is accompanied by a very southern, raspy accent.

No, no, no, no, I think, not again. I knew Ms. Broussard and Chad had opened investigations at the Board, but now Mr. and Mrs. Emerson have as well. Will this end?

"Good afternoon Mr. Barton, how may I help you?" I try to stifle my fear.

"Do you have time to answer some questions for me?"

"Absolutely. Did Mr. and Mrs. Emerson file a complaint with the Board?"

"Yes, ma'am, they did."

"Okay, I thought so and wanted to make sure." My heart sinks, and I am reminded how small and insignificant

I feel in the face of this problem.

"Ms. Tribb, you own the majority of Magnolia Maison, is that correct?"

"Yes, sir, I do. My partner Allie owns 20 percent," my voice shakes.

"Speaking of Ms. Marshall, she and I spoke earlier this week, and she is saying she never let you use her license for Magnolia Maison to pull permits."

"Whoa, whoa, whoa, what? That is a mistake. She and I own the business together."

"I understand that, Ms. Tribb. I am just letting you know what she's told me. If this is the case, we have a much bigger issue at hand."

I am speechless. Is Allie abandoning me, so she can get out of this and leave me on the hook alone?

"Ms. Tribb? Are you there?"

"Yes, sir, I'm trying to wrap my brain around what you've just said. Are you sure she understood the question?" I say, trying not to sound panicked, although I'm doing a terrible job at it.

"As far as I know, yes, ma'am."

"Do you mind if we put her on the phone with us? I want to get this cleared up right away."

"Sure thing, I'll wait."

I add a call and dial in Allie. Waiting on her to answer feels like hours. What if she doesn't answer?

"Hey, Audrey!"

"I have Victor Barton on the other line from St. Charles Parish. Can I put you on three-way with us?"

"Yeah," she sounds trepidatious.

I merge the calls together, "Mr. Barton, you still there?"

"Yes, ma'am, do you have Ms. Marshall on the phone?"

"I'm here," Allie says.

"Okay, Ms. Marshall, when we spoke on the phone earlier this week, did you state that you didn't consent to let Audrey or Magnolia Maison pull permits with your license?"

"No, sir, that's not what I said. You asked me if I had a contract in place with Magnolia Maison, which we don't. We have a verbal agreement for Magnolia Maison to use my license in exchange for 20 percent of the company."

"So, you're allowing Magnolia Maison and Audrey Tribb to use your license to pull permits, is that correct?"

"Yes," she replies.

"Do you mind sending me an email stating that, so I can

include this in my report?"

"Definitely. Is everything okay?" Allie sounds so far away. I want to give her a hug and smack her at the same time for almost giving me a heart attack. I can't help but worry about what would've happened if Mr. Barton hadn't called and clarified her statement.

"Mr. Barton scared me when he said you weren't allowing us to use your license," I say to Allie.

"We must have miscommunicated because that is not at all what I said. I'm sorry, Mr. Barton, if I wasn't clear before," Allie sounds defeated.

"That's alright. I'm just trying to clear all this up and give my report to the Board."

"Thank you so much for calling. Really, thank you, this could've turned out so differently if that ended up in your report."

Mr. Barton hangs up.

"Allie, are you still there?" I ask, hoping she hasn't hung up.

"Yeah, I'm here. What in the world was that? How could he have misunderstood what I said?" she asks almost incredulously.

"At first, I almost flew off the handle. I panicked, thinking you told him you didn't let us use your license."

"I would've too. You know me, though. I wouldn't do that to you."

"I know, but look at what we've been through so far. I'm at the point now that sometimes I don't know what to believe," I trail off.

"Gosh, I wish I didn't know how you felt. We're going to see this through to the end and then thrive, not just survive. I can see it, we're going to be okay, Audrey."

"I sure hope so. I feel like we just dodged a huge setback. The meeting is tomorrow, I'm hoping they'll give us the license, and we can get back to work. I can't come home until Ms. Broussard settles with us, so it's still a waiting game."

"Have you heard anything else from her?" she asks. I know she's as ready as I am to get this behind us.

"No, I haven't. I assumed since we accepted her terms that we'd hear back from her, but still nothing," I try not to sound hopeless.

"I wonder what the holdup is. Let me know if you do hear something."

"You know I will. Call me if anything else comes up, okay?" We need to be on the same page, and I hope she understands my meaning.

"You got it."

12

Friday morning, I wake early, my chest aching with anxiety. I have coffee with my devotionals and pray for God's will in this journey. If God wants to open the door for us to get our license, then He will make sure it happens. The house is quiet for now, and I think about all that stems from today. If they give us the license, then will the charge of interior design fraud be able to stand? Another question I need to send William. While it's on my mind, I draft a quick email, I need to know why we haven't heard from Ms. Broussard.

William,

Any word from Ms. Broussard or her attorney since we accepted her terms, so we can get these charges dropped?

Also, the Board is meeting today to accept or reject our application for the correct license. If they grant us the license, does this have any bearing on the current charges? Can they just go away or be dropped by the District Attorney since we would no longer be breaking the law?

Thanks,

Audrey

Now that I have that done, my mind wanders to Calvin Maxwell, my state representative, who never reached back out to me. I'll make it a point to call his office again today. At least if they can't help me, they should be able to tell me instead of wasting my time.

The Board will be meeting at nine this morning. I check their website one last time to make sure we still have everything complete in our application. All looks well. Earlier this week, I called the Board and asked how soon we'd find out about the license if they were meeting on Friday. They said that same afternoon. I'm relieved we'll know something today.

I need to keep my mind occupied for the remainder of the morning before I drive myself mad. Aunt Peggy suggests we go for a hike in the woods behind their house to search for pine knots since winter is coming. They have central heat and air but rarely ever use it. An old-fashioned, wood-burning stove sits cozily in the living room. I never really understood the value of pine knot until I had my own wood-burning fireplace. Pine knot can best be described as kindling on steroids. When a pine tree dies and falls, the pine sap that's left gathers into the dead branches and logs. It's concentrated and burns hot as if it were gasoline. Strike a match to rich pine knot, and it lights immediately. Aunt Peggy is the best pine knot hunter around. If it were a competition, she'd always win. She can tell just by looking at a piece of wood and can spot one from fifty feet, it's one of her many hidden talents. Probably came from a long line of gatherers.

A couple hours have passed, and we have a wagon full of rich-smelling pine knots as we head back for the house. We throw them in the pine knot pile next to the house so J. W. can chop them into small, burnable pieces. They treat it as if it were gold, never having a pine knot fire, only using it to start a fire. Otherwise, you're wasting it, and that is considered a sin in this part of Texas.

I've made it to 1:00 and can't contain it any longer, so I open the website and log in as I have so many times before, hoping this time the result will be different. Clicking on "Application Status," I wait for the page to load. A big green check sits beside our application. When I click on the application, it now offers the option to print the license. We did it! We have been approved! I quickly take a picture and send it to Allie. She sends tons of emojis relaying her excitement. I can't help but let out a loud, "YAY!" Now we have collateral and are within the confines of the law.

I send a copy of the license to William with the caption, "We are now officially licensed! Please advise on where we go from here."

Riding on the wave of excitement, I decide to call Calvin Maxwell's office.

"State Representative Calvin Maxwell's office, how may I help you?" the same sweet-voiced lady answers.

"Hi there, it's Audrey Tribb with Magnolia Maison again. The interior designer?"

"Oh, hi there, Ms. Tribb. Mr. Maxwell has had a very busy week, so I apologize he hasn't reached out to you. He had a lot to catch up on since he was gone for his son's wedding."

"I can imagine. Listen, I just wanted to let him know that the Board did grant us the correct license, but I was still wondering if he could help with these arrest warrants and how the Board handled this whole situation, especially their St. Tammany investigator, Sandy Colefield. From what I understand, she was out of line in aiding my client in filing arrest warrants as an employee of the Board."

"I completely understand, Ms. Tribb. I can't even imagine what you're going through," she sounds sympathetic. "This isn't formal advice, but have you thought about calling Louisiana's Attorney General's office? They govern the Interior Design Board and could help with Magnolia Maison not getting due process."

"The Attorney General's office? I didn't realize they governed the Board. I definitely will make sure to reach out to them. Thank you so much for that information."

Another piece of the puzzle and a step in the right direction. I'm sure the Attorney General's office can help more than State Representative Calvin Maxwell if they govern the Interior Design Board. More good news.

Audrey,

Still no word from Ms. Broussard's attorney.

Mr. Chad Ewing's attorney has drawn up the settlement papers that you need to come in and sign. Let me know when you can be here to sign them, so we can get that one knocked out. I'm free Tuesday afternoon.

William

There are so many reasons I need to go home and the one obvious reason I don't. Chad won't drop the charges until I've signed the settlement papers, his collateral. It's a huge risk to go home and sign these papers, but one I might be willing to take.

I've talked it over with my parents and told them my plan. I'd leave Jasper Tuesday morning, drive to New Orleans, pick some things up from my house, and sign the papers at William's office. A one-day trip and then head back to Aunt Peggy and J. W.'s house until the charges are dropped.

Part of me is excited about movement in the right direction. I need to get something accomplished, so I start packing and preparing for my trip, detailing exactly how

Tuesday will go. I don't even want to know how full my mailbox is.

So many people pray over my safety on this trip. Laura, Aunt Peggy, I'm sure even J. W., and my parents. My mom isn't crazy about me traveling alone while the arrest warrants are still active, but I tell her it's something I need to do. We all know the risk I'm taking, but in order to settle with Chad, I have to go.

Tuesday morning, I'm up at 4:00, ready to leave for New Orleans. J. W. is already up and has prepared me a coffee to go.

He looks at me sternly and says, "You drive two under the speed limit, complete stop at all stop signs, and keep your eyes peeled. No textin' and drivin' ya hear?"

"Yes, sir," I grin at him.

He's not the hugging type, but he wraps me in a bear hug as I hear Aunt Peggy coming down the hall.

"Audrey, are you sure this is what you want to do? You know what could happen," she says, half pleading.

"Yes, ma'am, I have to sign these papers, so we can move forward. I know this isn't how I saw it happening either, but at least I can get one settlement knocked out," I say, trying to sound convincing.

"If that's what you think, then we will pray for you until you get back. Please call us and let us know how things are goin'," she says as she hugs me.

They wave from the front porch and watch me leave. It's going to be a long day in the car. I need to stay focused, get my business done, and get back here. I wish Ms. Broussard's attorney would've had the settlement documents ready, so I could get both done at once. The threat more minimal that way, but I'll have to take what I can get.

The trip is four and a half hours and is mostly uneventful by hour two. When I hit the Louisiana state line, my anxiety is heightened. Are they out looking for me? I keep my eyes trained on the rear-view mirror, set my cruise two under the speed limit, and pray I make it safely.

I decide to run by my house first since it's on the way and William isn't going to be in the office until 9:00. I need to check the mail and grab some warmer clothes. Driving to my house feels like it always has, but I wonder if anyone's camped out down the street waiting on me.

As I make the final turn to my house, I see that the street is empty. I let out a breath I didn't realize I'd been holding and check the mail. I pull into the garage and shut it. My hands ache as I take them off the steering wheel. I must've been tenser than I thought. Even though no one saw me come in, I'm still nervous about being here. Everything looks as it did when I left for Mia's wedding all those weeks ago. I didn't anticipate that I wouldn't be back right away. Quickly, I grab another small suitcase and fill it with jackets, jeans, and sweatshirts. The weather is getting colder, and I'm tired of shorts and the same pair of yoga pants.

Finally, I throw my suitcase in the trunk and head for William's office. Sitting at the stoplight next to my neighborhood, my eye catches a car sitting across from me at the intersection. I realize it's a police car which I find immediately odd. Police cars are rarely ever out here, only sheriffs because it's out of the city limits. I decide to drive straight instead of turning to go to William's office. As the light changes, time seems to have slowed. We pass each other, I look closely at the driver, and my stomach drops. Chad. Things suddenly come full speed, and I panic.

My heart begins to pound out of my chest, and I start crying. I didn't know fear until now. I look in my rear-view mirror, and he's turned around and now chasing after me, lights and siren off. My eyes flit from the speedometer to the road, keeping to the speed limit because he can't pull me over without probable cause. Luckily there is a car between us, but I can see him crossing the double yellow line making sure I'm still here. I don't even know what to do or where to go.

Turning into a neighborhood, I see him behind me make another U-turn in the middle of the road. He's going away from me now—the thought of what just happened slams into my chest. I start gagging and sobbing. Why is he doing this? The look on his face was one I've never seen before. The Chad I knew never looked like that. His nice face now distorted with rage and hate. I can't sit here anymore, so I also turn around. I'm so mad that he can use his patrol car to stalk and terrify me. The grocery store is about three miles down the road. A parking lot I know that will keep me hidden until I decide what to do. Who can I call when I feel unsafe? Obviously not the police.

I park between two trucks and call William's office.

"Hey, Audrey, what's going on?"

I can't even catch my breath, "You won't believe what just happened! I was driving to your office from my house, and I passed by Chad, right by my neighborhood! In his police car!"

"Can you get here?" he quickly replies.

"I'm not sure anymore. I want to go back to Jasper. I was coming in to sign these papers for him, and he's skulking around my neighborhood trying to catch me? I am now questioning his motive. There are never police officers out here. He lives an hour in the opposite direction, you can't tell me he was patrolling out here! He has no family out here. The only reason why he's out here is to intimidate and check if I'm here. This is sick. I think *I'm* going to be sick. Isn't that illegal for him to be doing personal business in his patrol car? Not to mention all the laws he just broke by following me." My brain has finally caught up, and I'm angry and scared. Originally, I thought he just wanted his money back, now I fear he wants more than that.

"Well, we could file a complaint with the police department, but I really want to wait until after the settlements are complete to do anything like that. Listen, I know you're terrified and upset, but let's not let that cloud our judgment of what we need to do. Let's keep to the same plan. We can figure this out after the settlements are complete." I can tell he's trying to keep me calm, but right now, the way Chad just took control because he's a police officer infuriates me.

"No," I say firmly. "I'm not coming in to sign those papers. I'm going to wait until Ms. Broussard has her settlement papers ready, then I'll be in to sign them both. I'm not coming back until they're ready. It's not my fault Chad can't act as an adult. He's gone too far, and I don't trust the guy even more now. He wants me to be arrested, what kind of twisted man would do that to someone he knows? I'm his son's age! I could be his kid! He *knows* I didn't do any of this on purpose, yet he is treating me like a common criminal."

My body is shaking violently. I won't be persuaded by William to stay and give Chad what he wants while he intimidates me with his badge and police car. Underneath that uniform, he's a human being who's not above the law and shouldn't be taking it into his own hands. I'm held to the highest standard for my business and not breaking the law. How is he allowed to as a police officer? Chad isn't above the law, and if he's not careful, he'll find himself in my shoes.

I call my mom and cry uncontrollably. She never once says she told me so or that this is the risk I was willing to take. She prays protection over me and agrees I should head back to Jasper. She'll call Aunt Peggy and let her know. I am now running scared, and he knows it. Check! Mission accomplished, Chad. Ugh, I'm so aggravated I could scream.

On my drive back to Jasper, I can't stop thinking about what Chad did. What would possess him to lurk around my neighborhood searching for me? The thought unnerves me even more now. If I'm arrested, God only knows what would happen to me then. I need to get across the state line to Texas and out of Louisiana as fast as the speed limit will let me.

A few hours down the road, a memory pops into my brain as I'm replaying what happened with Chad. When I was in high school, I heard what I always assumed was a rumor that Chad, or Mr. Ewing at the time, had a charge of domestic assault against his wife. At the time, I brushed it away, number one because it wasn't my business and number two because I couldn't imagine Mr. Ewing being guilty of that because he's a police officer. Of course, it never came to a conviction. After seeing his face being distorted with rage, I found anything to be believable at this point.

The truth is stranger than fiction.

I'm emotionally worn out by the time I pull onto Aunt Peggy and J. W.'s dirt lane. I sit in the car quietly, praying and trying to understand how this got out of hand so quickly.

"Why, God? Why is this happening? I'm trying to do what You will for me. I'm trying to make all this right. Why can't they see that? I know You're in control, but right now, I'm having a hard time moving forward. I want to quit. I'm not brave or strong without You. Please be with me and give me Your guidance on where I go from here."

13

I'm still in shock several days later. My brain cannot process at this point. I lie around and don't do much of anything when I get back to Jasper. Worse news came with an email from William. Apparently, getting the appropriate license solved nothing in the way of getting the charges dropped. Since we entered into contracts with Ms. Broussard and Chad with the wrong license initially, everything remains the same. I feel beat up and hopeless. What is the point anymore?

I begin journaling my true thoughts. On the outside, however, I tell everyone I talk to that it's going to be okay, and we will just continue with the settlements. It'll all work out. I wish I believed half of what I said. Seems other people are buying it.

My people-pleasing tendencies are being tested. Take a people-pleaser and put her in a situation where she can't please people and watch her every belief come crashing down. The thought crosses my mind that I'm not supposed to please people, and maybe that's where the lesson needs to be learned. I should be living for an audience of One. All I want is peace. So that's what I pray for. Peace that only He can provide. Not that any medication, TV show, social media post, or drink can ease. The pain I have can only be healed through Him.

I begin spending more time praying and reading my Bible. Habakkuk, David's Psalms, and of course, Job, among so many others who faced persecution. Before, I couldn't relate because I didn't know true pain and heartache. But now? These prophets are my kindred spirits. The lens I now see the world through has changed. My belief in humanity has been rocked to my core, and I'm jaded. I never understood the mind of a pessimist. Maybe those pessimists have been hurt so badly they can't see the good in the world anymore.

Laura has been sending me random songs now and then with an accompanying text like, "heard this and thought of you!" She's my tether to the real world when I feel I'm in a dark hole. When I don't feel like praying or reading my Bible, I'll get a text from her reminding me of God's goodness. I'm in awe of her obedience to God's voice. However, she's always the one saying how proud she is of my bravery; the problem is I don't feel brave. I'm scared. As humans, fear is natural. To have faith in God and put all your trust in Him can be scary but completely worth it in the end.

Finally, I decide to go through my mail. I've been avoiding it. I sit on the bed, creating shred, junk, and open piles. One envelope catches my eye, marked from the New Orleans District Attorney's office. I don't have any clients in New Orleans Parish. I rip the envelope open and quickly scan the contents of the letter. Mr. Emerson's name pops out at me, accompanied with the hot check division. Why in the world would I get this letter? Wait, I lent some money to the Emerson's when they were going through a rough patch. My checking account hasn't alerted me of insufficient funds. I decide to double check anyway. Nearly a month ago, the check was returned to my bank. I re-read the letter. There will be an arrest warrant issued if I don't pay the amount of the check in ten days. I must've missed this in my personal account since I was out of town and partially out of my mind. He should've told me, and I would've figured out how to make it right. What is wrong with people?

Now I have to figure out how to pay this to the District Attorney's office in two days. Everything is forcing me to go back home and handle business. No one else's name is on my account, and the District Attorney wants a cashier's check complete with a hefty fee. All anyone wants is money. Most people get that verse wrong in the Bible about money. They think "money is the root of all evil" is how it goes, but it really reads, "*love* of money is the root of all evil." Money by itself is just that, pieces of cotton paper, but what it can get you is what people love.

Thanksgiving came and went. The day was spent like

most families across America, watching football and eating too many helpings of mashed potatoes and gravy. I feel so far away and disconnected. I'm ready to go home and back to normal if there ever will be a normal after this. William finally forwarded the acceptance settlement from Ms. Broussard. I wanted to set a date right away, but I still haven't heard anything. It's been a week since I requested a date to sign the settlement papers. Why is she stalling? My fear is that she doesn't have the funds to settle. Regardless, I need to have this behind me.

More and more, I begin to miss home. I need to go home and take care of this hot check before another warrant is issued in another parish. My dad offers his home in his gated community in New Orleans. There are guards outside both entry gates, so I know no one can just drive by and see I'm there. The thought begins to blossom, and now I want to go home more than ever. Ultimately my family says it's my decision, except Aunt Peggy. She really doesn't want me going considering what happened last time. My dad says I can come anytime. I know he misses me. Feeling like the settlements are close to being wrapped up, I decide to leave that Friday and just pray it all works out.

Friday morning, my anxiety is high, but I continue packing my bags. I can see the worry in Aunt Peggy's eyes as she wraps me in a hug.

She lightly whispers, "Let me know when you get there. Please keep your head on a swivel and know that you can always come back. We're going to miss you, girl."

"Yes, ma'am. Thank you for all you've done for me." I say, pulling away. "I'll call you when I stop for gas and make sure to let you know when I get to my dad's."

Again, J. W. sends me off with a bear hug. Even J. W. is worried, and if he is worried, I begin to wonder if I'm making the right decision.

The drive back to New Orleans is smooth and uneventful, mainly because I set my cruise to one under the speed limit and use my blinker religiously. I need to get a cashier's check from the bank first. Then I'll go to my dad's house.

Using the back entrance of the neighborhood, I take the winding roads and finally reach the place I used to call home. I can still see in my mind the two pine trees that we removed a decade ago. They blocked the view of the house and littered the front yard with pine needles. Now sits a clear view of the house with a sweeping front porch complete with hanging ferns. You'd be hard-pressed to find a southern porch without ferns. They blissfully sway in the breeze catching the sun periodically when they peek out from under the protection of shade. The neighborhood is quiet save a few birds chirping their afternoon song. Fall is making its mark here too.

My stepmom comes out to greet me and to help carry in my bags. She suggests I park in the garage just in case, an offer I willingly accept. After I'm settled in the guest bedroom, she and I sit on the back patio that overlooks the golf course. The room I stayed in from high school has been turned into my stepmom's craft room. It's been ten years since I've lived here, but it still reminds me of home.

My parents are wealthy, but only because they're smart with their money. I've made a mental promise to be obedient and tithe 10 percent when this is all over. Tithing is an act of obedience and doesn't mean I won't run into any more problems, but my financial problems will ease. Giving back to God a fraction of what He's given me is what I should have been doing all along.

"The ferns are still so beautiful," I start.

"It's almost time for me to bring them inside," she says quietly. She changes tack quickly, "Your dad is worried about you, Audrey."

I take a deep breath. The last thing I want to do is disappoint anyone, especially my family. "I know. Sometimes I think this never happened. But I'm hoping that once the settlements are signed, the District Attorney will drop the charges soon after. I don't know what to expect anymore."

"Did you ever hear from the Attorney General's office?"

"Yeah, they said they couldn't help me. Since the Board didn't bring the charges against us, then they don't see how I have any case against them."

"What are your plans this week?"

"I'm scheduled to sign settlement papers next Friday for Chad. I still haven't heard back about Ms. Broussard's settlement papers. Hopefully, I can at least get Chad's settlement signed and out of the way so the District Attorney can drop the charges."

"Are those the terms? That the District Attorney will drop the charges as long as you let him out of the contract?"

"No, Chad, '*the victim*,' has to drop the charges, and we *hope* that the Jefferson District Attorney wants to as well."

The worst part of the deal has been revealed. I've finally said it aloud, and it hurts as much as I thought it would. We were accused of a felony. We were forced to settle with the threat of being arrested hanging over our heads, all for the District Attorney to hopefully drop the charges. How backward.

"So, you have to settle, and the District Attorney may not even drop the charges? And you can't go to civil court because you'll have to pay Chad's attorney fees and yours all to prove you're innocent?" She sounds as baffled and frustrated as I feel. "It sounds like you have no leverage and no fighting chance."

"That's exactly how I feel. Completely defeated."

We sit in silence while the reality of what I've just said sits in the crisp fall air between us. I'm unsure of what she's thinking, but I don't see a way out of this. Not a way that doesn't take a long time to dissolve. I was hoping in weeks we would settle this. Now it's looking like months. Chad, Ms. Broussard, or Mr. Emerson never came to me. I'd like to think that we could've avoided all of this and settled out of court. They reacted out of emotion, and now they've delayed their projects being done. How was this the only way they felt they could go about handling this? It all circles back around to Ms. Broussard. She doesn't have the money to pay us and was trying to get out of it entirely. This was her way, and she needed help to do it. They thought we'd be jailed and convicted guilty, all while she got to sit in her newly remodeled home debt-free while I sat in a jail cell. The anger envelops my heart like acid, burning and gnawing at my insides with nowhere to go.

"We have our license now, so we really need to continue on Mr. Emerson's project this week before he decides to do something crazy too."

"Would he file charges too, you think?"

"Honestly, I believe he would. The awful things he's sent me over the last month have shocked me, so at this point, yes, I believe he would."

The reality of my last sentence is heavy and stark. Finally, she sighs, "I better figure out what we're going to have for supper before your brother and dad get home," she says as she heads inside.

After she leaves, I sit on the patio a few moments longer, letting the fall sun hit my face. I close my eyes and rest my head. The damning thoughts can be so loud even in this quiet space. They're deafening with shouts of, "You should be ashamed of yourself!" and "Who are you kidding? You knew you couldn't succeed at this" oh and my favorite, "You're a joke, everyone knows it, and they knew only something like this could happen to you, you can't get your life together." I'm beginning to become worn down by the whole situation. My prayers are the only thing I hold onto anymore. I still pray for peace. That's all I can do anymore. Months of chronic stress and anxiety can't be good for the body. I silently pray for this to be over soon.

14

The following week I spend most of the time answering emails and returning phone calls trying to determine the future of Magnolia Maison. Right now, I can't see past the end of my nose to continue doing new business. We never had a physical office; we hadn't gotten that far yet, so we ran the majority of day-to-day business out of my house. We've temporarily shut down, only working out of the guest bedroom in my dad's house. Allie and I work out a timeline for finishing Mr. Emerson's project. We begin work on Tuesday. She and I agree that it's not smart to visit his home while all this is going on. We set up appointments for work to be done at his home without us being there to look over the project.

I become comfortable in my surroundings, driving in the guise of my brother's car. I try to check my mail once a day. I don't want to run the risk of missing anything important. It's risky, but I begin to believe that they're not looking for me at all. Chad was on his own that day, not at the instruction of the New Orleans Police Department. He was running his own personal errand that day. I began to separate the two and thought Chad would stay away, considering the risk of him jeopardizing his career with police malfeasance was too high. Surely he's guilty of that on more than one occasion. But again, I doubt I'll get any support against a police officer.

The night before we're set to settle with Chad, I get an email from William. The ominous and familiar ding instantly causes my heart to race. I'm Pavlov's dog, the email notification is the bell, but instead of a reward, I get bad news. I make a mental note to either switch from Outlook or change the notification tone. It seems Chad's attorney has canceled and moved the settlement date to after Christmas. Again, my spirit is deflated. One would think I'd be used to this feeling by now, but I'm not. It astounds me that people search for it in amusement parks, that sudden drop in the pit of your stomach. I've always hated that feeling. Maybe I should tell them they can get it for free, just do business with the wrong people and get a bonus to the adrenaline—despair. I thought Chad wanted this over, and I begin to wonder whether this was all a setup to get me back in Louisiana. He knew I'd have to come back to physically sign.

When people recount a life-altering moment, they can typically detail all the events leading up to it. I cannot. The best way to describe these past few months is that I've experienced an intense brain fog. My mind has shut out anything except the awful things and news I've gotten. That's how our brains are wired, aren't they? We remember the insults and forget the compliments. We forget the good.

I don't remember all I did that Friday I was arrested. I do remember it was a pretty day, uncharacteristically warmer than normal, but it typically is for a Louisiana winter. This was supposed to be the day we settled with Chad. I just remember pizza and popcorn under the twinkling lights of the Christmas tree. Now I'm sitting downtown surrounded by concrete and strangers, wondering if this wasn't the plan all along. To humiliate and break me with three counts of interior design fraud. Turns out Mr. Emerson did file charges even when we were working to complete his project. The devil is afoot, especially in those whose hearts are pliable and ready for the taking.

As I wait for lights out, the electric hum reverberates my bones.

"Baker! Get your things and come on."

Robin quickly rolls her mattress and shouts a gleeful goodbye to us. I envy her for getting out of these four walls, but I, like her, will just be transported to another jail, she to Texas me to another parish. A steppingstone into another dismal room, but still a step closer to freedom.

Hours later, when the room is quiet and everyone is asleep, I lie awake, my head pounding, trying to organize my thoughts into rational ones. An unnerving thought begins to form. I have the uncanny feeling of being watched. What if these guards are taking pictures of me in my orange, curled in the fetal position, and sending them to him? Is this what he wants, complete and utter shame? The thought makes me shudder, and I push it away. There's nothing I can do about it right now. Hanging on to God's promises and that justice will prevail, I close my eyes and pray myself to sleep.

Sunday morning is the same as Saturday was. Typically, after the 6:00 breakfast, everyone is allowed to go back to bed. This morning I decided to sit on the bench and read the Bible. It's quieter in the mornings when everyone is still asleep. I start to worry that Jefferson Parish won't pick me up anytime soon, so I try to keep a routine. Routine is warranted in a place like this. As I brush my teeth, I realize how greasy my hair is beginning to look. If I can see it in the blurred image looking back at me, then I know it's bad. Not that I care, but being cleaner would make me feel better. There's a shower in the corner of the room. Some women took showers last night. I might be brave enough to tonight. A piece of thin, plastic tarp is allowed to be duct-taped as a make-shift shower door, and they only shower one at a time. I'm thankful for that. Trying to remember the last time I showered, I decide I'm definitely going to.

The mood is quieter today and more somber. There's an air about the room that feels hopeless, and it's catching—no transports and no court on Sundays, which means no hope of anyone getting out today. Yesterday the room was electric, filled with movement and laughter. They've turned the TV on, and a marathon of some reality show consumes our day. We watch someone else's drama to take our minds off our own. The ironies never cease. Our lives aren't as glamorous but much more dramatic than any writer could create. The intricacies of life that bring us here and connect us are our identity.

Last night my mom told me Laura was planning on visiting me today, which gives me mixed feelings. I'm not sure I can take anyone I know seeing me like this. Not that I have much choice, I resign and accept that she's coming, and I let myself look forward to it. The door buzzes, and I half-expect them to call my name because Laura is here. Instead, there are two guards, one with medicine, the other to hold the door. After all the medicine is distributed, I decide to be brave. I am human, after all, and I *think* I'm allowed to ask a question.

"Can I have some Tylenol?" I ask the guard holding the door.

"Do I look like I have medicine!?" she shouts at me. I've never felt more like a child in my entire life than I do now. I wasn't sure the humiliations could get worse. Obviously, I was wrong.

Hours pass, and my head is splitting. Very little water

and no food doesn't help the caffeine headache that threatens to rip my skull in two—still, no sign of Laura.

"Hey Momma, have you heard from Laura? She hasn't shown..."

"Ask her what time it is!" Tiffany shouts at my back.

"Oh, umm, what time is it?" I ask my mom.

"Hold on," I can hear her distantly rustling her phone away from her face, so she can see what time it is. I can imagine her sitting on her couch in the living room, peering down the end of her nose through her glasses, trying to read the time. She always cozies up in the corner of the couch nearest the lamp and typically huddled under a thick blanket, which she kicks off every forty-five minutes because of a hot flash. Apparently, not only does jail not have clocks, neither do homes anymore. "It's 4:36."

"4:36!" I shout back to the room and to no one in particular. I know Tiffany isn't the only one curious to know. It's a rite of passage and common knowledge now that if you're on the phone, prepare to be interrupted mid-sentence for someone to ask the time. Reminds me of a meerkat randomly popping up in a serious conversation to ask the time.

"They won't let Laura visit you, honey," my mom gently breaks the news.

"Why not?" I scoff.

"Since you're a fugitive, they won't allow any visitors."

Her words hit me hard in the chest. I wonder again if this is Chad or typical protocol. Fugitive. The word elicits an image of someone in a high-speed car chase actually running from the police. Since I didn't turn myself in right away, I guess the definition fits. It's hard looking back knowing if I made the right decision not to turn myself in. Terrified, no money for bail, and unfairly charged. I really thought the charges would've been dropped by now. No point having regrets for the decisions I've made. I can't change it. I need to focus on moving forward and getting out of this.

Anger has taken root as the hopelessness of my situation settles in. People will write me off because I've been charged with a felony, and my legacy is stained. What will later be a scar is now an open and bleeding wound that I try to rationalize and make sense of. I hate this place.

Dinner was awful again. All I can remember was the cornbread—so much bread. Lukewarm sink water and lemon sandwich cookies are all I've eaten since Friday. I'm not even close to being hungry, my nerves won't allow it. Thinking of tomorrow helps pass the time. If Jefferson Parish comes to get me tomorrow, then hopefully, St. Charles Parish and St. Tammany won't be far behind. What a long road I still have. I've finally gotten to know some ladies in here, and the thought of having to reacquaint myself three more times nauseates me.

After our showers, Tiffany, Denisha, and I gather the ladies for a prayer circle. All but the woman in yellow participates. We sat on the bunks in the back, some standing, some sitting, and we all held hands. I prayed over these women and asked God for their protection and quick release. It was a divine moment. I could feel God's presence as I asked for their children to be blessed and safe while their mommas were here. None of these women were evil, but all made mistakes. They wanted desperately to be home for Christmas with their families. We all knew that Monday would be a telling day and one of change. Not all of us would be here tomorrow. Who would get out, be transported, or have to stay? There wasn't a dry eye when we finished. God was there, and I silently thanked Him for being a comfort for those who needed Him.

15

Almost everyone woke for breakfast Monday morning and waited for the day to begin. The anxiety of waiting was murderous. The sun finally came up, and the minute the phones turned on, they were buzzing with activity. I had no one to call about my release. I was waiting on Jefferson Parish, silently pleading to be on to the next step of this horrific journey.

"Roll call! Roll call! Roll call!"

Another day in here was unthinkable. I began to pray out loud as we waited on the sergeant.

"God, I praise you and thank You for all You've done for me. I know without a shadow of a doubt that You are in contr—"

The hum of the electric door cut me off. It wasn't the sergeant but a male guard.

"Tribb! Get your things and come on!"

My knees gave way, and my heart leaps. Jefferson Parish was here, and I was getting out of this place.

"Thank you, God!" I said as I frantically rolled up my mattress and grabbed my "belongings."

As we walked down what I originally thought was such a long hall that first night, seemed so short today. I put my tattered mattress back in the storage room, not looking back. I was given my clothes and told to dress quickly. Where I undressed that scary first night, I put my own clothes back on. It felt so good to be in my jeans and dirty socks again.

I was placed in a locked waiting room as the other inmates were dressing. My elation was quickly replaced when I saw the mammoth of a man who I presumed was the sheriff from Jefferson Parish here to transport us. He must've been over six feet tall with a shaved head and dark blue polyester uniform. Intimidating doesn't begin to describe how he looks.

"Ma'am, please step over to this wall with your hands behind your back," he said gruffly.

I walked quietly and quickly as he instructed.

"She's headed to St. Charles and St. Tammany parishes when she's done in Jefferson," said the overweight New Orleans City Police sergeant behind the desk.

"Man, she's been busy, hasn't she?" the Jefferson Parish sheriff replied.

They talk about me as if I'm not here. This is exactly what I feared. They assume I'm guilty and have no idea what I've been through. I want to scream or explain, but instead, I stand there with my head hung, letting them openly judge me like an animal.

Since I'm a female, a New Orleans City female guard has to search me for him. My back pockets still don't open. I awkwardly try to explain.

She turns me around, and then the Jefferson sheriff approaches with handcuffs. Two on my hands and two on my feet. If my heart could sink any lower, it would leave my body. Shame abounds. He helps me into the van and places me on the front bench seat.

"No talking. We have a long drive."

"Yes, sir," I say.

He places two other male inmates near the back and tells us all not to talk to each other. I don't know who I feel safer with, the cop or the inmates. My mind is still at war with my new reality.

The drive was incredibly long. But when I heard last night from the other women that they were most likely taking me to the maximum-security prison, I didn't know what to expect. Forty minutes later, we pulled into Gretna, and from outside appearances, the prison seemed well-kept. As we entered the single garage and the automatic door closed, my heart began to race. What was I walking into now?

Another waiting room at the front of the jail. A tall counter that made a square. At the back, they booked inmates, and at the front, they posted bond with visitors. I was waved up first to be booked in. A short man with a boyish figure and glasses started the booking-in process again. Taking in my surroundings, the atmosphere seemed happy and light. Whereas New Orleans City Jail was dark and ominous. I didn't know how to process this. He placed me in an individual cell with an automatic door that closed.

Several minutes later, I was allowed to make a phone call.

My dad answered on the second ring.

"Hey honey, is everything okay?"

"I made it to Jefferson Parish. Are you able to meet Charles here to bond me out so St. Charles Parish can come and get me?"

"Yes, let me call Charles and see what we can do."

"Okay, thank you. There are real murderers in here, Daddy. I'm nervous. Once we hang up, I can't call back."

"I'll get Charles up there, and we'll post the bond today."

They let me walk myself back to my cell. At least they're kind and treat me like a human. My door opens again several minutes later.

"Ms. Tribb?" A woman about my age asks. She's obviously a guard.

"Yes?"

"Please come with me, so we can get you into the clothes you'll be wearing while you're here," she says pleasantly. I would think this was a nice place of business on any other day. But I can't forget the reason I'm really here. While this isn't Chad's place of employment, this is the parish he lives in, and he is a police officer. I assume they stick together.

We walk to a closed room, and I'm given all new clothes: off-white sports bra and underwear, which I gladly accept since I haven't changed mine since Friday. That was the worst part after my shower last night, putting on my same undergarments. No orange jumpsuits this time, but a faded red and white striped shirt and pants set with a white T-shirt underneath. Rubber slippers and no socks. She leads me back to the holding cell while I wait and watch for what comes next. I have full view of the lobby and visitors coming and going. I've never met Charles, so I don't know who I'm looking for to post my bond. An hour goes by, and my door slides open again. This time a man in khaki slacks and a tie stands at the threshold.

"Ms. Tribb, please come with me," he says as he turns around with his clipboard in hand.

We walk to a closed interview room, and he offers me a seat across from him.

"I'm Detective Anderson investigating your case. Is

it alright if I ask you a couple of questions? You are more than welcome to request your attorney be present." He has a kind disposition and doesn't seem much older than me. His belly protrudes a little, and he has an average man's haircut coupled with a baby face and no facial hair.

I probably should've taken more time to answer, but I had nothing to hide and was gladly ready to share my side of the story. Waiting for William to show up for an interview on the off-chance he's available wasn't a risk I was willing to take.

"Yes, I'd like to talk about what happened."

"Okay, can you start off by telling me the business you have with Mr. Chad Ewing? This conversation is recorded, and if this goes to trial, Mr. Ewing will be able to have access to it."

The thought of being able to talk to Chad directly emboldens me. If no one else is going to stand up for me, then I better do it. I re-tell exactly how I know Chad and the contract we had in place for his project, making sure to emphasize that the project was at cost. I only tell the facts. As I continue to talk, I can't help but cry. Thinking about this mountain of a problem I'm facing, I'm overcome and can't stop. He offers me a tissue and consoles me.

"I just don't understand why Chad is doing this. I've been praying that all this would go away. I just want peace," I sob.

He mentions as an aside that he, too, is a Christian and feels that I got caught up in something way over my head. Hearing this is a relief—finally, a human with some empathy. After a ten-minute conversation, he walks me back to my cell. I feel like he heard me and that I was honest about everything. We don't get three steps out of the interview room that Detective Anderson begins acting differently and slows his pace.

He talks under his breath, "To be honest, Audrey, I freaking hate Chad Ewing."

I can't catch my breath. Did I hear him right?

He continues, "Yeah, he really wanted me to arrest you, but I was going to wait until after the holidays. He kept harassing me with harsh phone calls at night. I'm trying to eat dinner with my family, and here's Chad calling again. The night you were arrested, he called me and wanted me to interview you that night. It pissed me off. I was inherited this case. I never would've brought charges against you for something like this."

He finishes as we stop at my cell. How can I convey how thankful I am for his honesty?

"I knew God would place someone in my path that would finally listen and believe me. Thank you."

The door closes, and I can't contain my excitement. The one person who's investigating me is on my side! Talk about a victory. I needed this so badly. Thank you, God, for Your provision! Finally, I feel like I can take a deep breath and rest in knowing that God is protecting me. God forgive me for ever doubting You.

I grab the Bible the woman guard let me have and begin praying and thanking God. What must have been an hour so later, my cell opens again and for the final time. The female guard says it's time to head to general population. Jesus, help me through this difficult walk. I know you're here holding my hand and walking beside me as I walk into what I'm unsure of.

There are two other women walking with us. I'm in the back assessing them. One has fried hair from being bleached too many times and smeared makeup. I saw her come in wearing a jean mini skirt. The amount of flirting she was doing with the officers made me uncomfortable, so I remind myself to not join forces with her.

The second and more timid woman is over forty-five and seems to know the blonde woman. Again, I am out here unaware and isolated. We stop at a closed door and wait while the female guard opens it. I hang behind, waiting for instructions because I can't hear what she's telling the other two. Then the contents of the room bring me back foldable mattresses. The other two women grab theirs, and I walk in to get mine.

The female guard follows me and whispers, "Make

sure to pick a good one, not one with holes. Get that one," she says as she points to a full-looking mattress under two holey ones. "I don't care what those girls get, just wanted to make sure you had a good one."

What she says floors me again. She keeps calling me "Ms. Tribb" and not even referencing the two other women at all. God's blessings are all around if I just look for them.

She tells me to wait while she walks the other two women to A-pod, not sure the significance of the different pods.

"I saw you reading a Bible in your holding cell earlier," the female guard says on her way back to me. "I am putting you in B-pod with a cellmate I think you'll get along with."

Processing what she's said, I hope she's not being sarcastic, but nothing leads me to believe she's lying. The huge sliding door opens, and the area is desolate. I can hear lots of voices, so what I can gather is that they're locked into their cells while I come in. I'm unable to assess how many women are in this pod. We walk all the way to the back-left corner and into an open cell marked B-109. The room is very small, with the square sink sitting over the toilet. A tall, thin window makes up the back wall, and the obvious two bunks make up the left wall. In the right corner sit two metal stools connected to a small metal table. I'm sure you could get this kind of property for a steep price in New York.

As soon as we enter, a woman pops out from the bottom bunk, and I immediately realize she's barely over four feet tall. Her hair is long and brown, and she's smiling with soft freckles covering her cheeks.

"I thought you two might get along well when I saw Ms. Tribb reading her Bible," the female guard says to the woman.

I can tell from their energy that they've known each other for a while and have developed a friendship. This female guard has gone out of her way to not only let me have a comfortable mattress but also took the time to place me with a cellmate I'd be compatible with. Thank you, Lord, for this guard.

"Hi, I'm Laura," she reaches out her hand for me to shake.

"I'm Audrey, nice to meet you," I say, taking her hand.

The female guard leaves, and the sound of the door slamming closed doesn't escape me. I try to focus my attention on getting to know Laura.

"My best friend's name is Laura."

"Oh, wow, that's awesome," she genuinely responds.

"How long have you been here?" I ask, trying to break the ice.

She gives a slight laugh, "What day is it?" She asks as

she looks over at her well-worn calendar. "Umm, I've been here since March 9th." She's very confident, laid back, and well-spoken, so I wonder why she's here.

How am I supposed to respond appropriately? If I act shocked, it will only remind her how awful her situation is. And if I respond nonchalantly, she'll think I am not interested. I decide for a mixture of both.

"Goodness, that must be tough."

"Where are you coming from?" she asks in turn.

"It's quite a long story. I own an interior design company, and my partner had the wrong license. Needless to say, operating without the right one is a felony. Three of my clients got in touch with each other, and the dominoes fell from there. They're all in separate parishes, so I'm having to post bond at each place, then wait to be transported. The worst part is a former friend of mine was a client and is a New Orleans City Police Officer, so there's that."

Her turn to be shocked. "What?!"

"Yeah, I'm glad to be out of New Orleans City Jail, his territory. It's awful over there."

"Yes, I've heard horror stories of that place. Jefferson isn't too bad. The guards are nice enough save a few."

"I'm relieved to hear that."

I turn to take in my surroundings and notice a name tag

hanging on the towel holder. It's a picture of Laura, but her name is listed as "Laura Tribb."

"Your last name is Tribb?"

"My maiden name is Tribb. It's Moss now, why?"

"You won't believe this; my last name is Tribb! Audrey Anne Tribb."

"Whoa, my full name is Laura Anne Tribb! Were we like adopted or something? There's no way this is a coincidence."

"You're telling me. That's unbelievable!"

"Where's your family from?" she quickly asks.

"My mom is from Colorado, but my dad is from Indiana."

"Huh, well, my family is from California, so I don't see how we could be related. It's just so crazy that this is happening," she says as she braids her hair behind her back.

Over the course of our conversation, I learn she reads many devotionals and has a lot of friends in here. She seems well-liked, and her energy is contagious. And she's happy even in these circumstances. Last March, her much older boyfriend was busted for crystal meth, and Laura happened to be there with him. He blamed the drugs on her, and they both went to jail because of it. Even though she barely looks thirty-five, Laura has two adult children and three grandbabies. Before jail, her life was typical, married with children and manager of a chain restaurant. After leaving her husband for reasons she wouldn't share, she got mixed up with the wrong crowd and started using drugs. My heart broke for her as she detailed how proud she was of her kids and the people they've grown up to be.

Collectively, all the doors open, and we're allowed to come out of our cells and into the common area. Trying to take in my new surroundings, I'm immediately taken by the vastness of the room. Two stories tall, the interior resembles the outside of a motel—all the doors on the outside leading to interior rooms. Two stairwells sit adjacent and parallel to each other, leading up to the second-floor cells. Black railing lines the walkway in a u-shape. Dozens of round metal tables sit methodically in the center of the massive room. Just like New Orleans City Jail, the guard's control room sits high, overlooking the common area behind tinted windows.

The energy in the room is full of laughter, and it shocks my system. I sit with Laura at a table with four stools, and we're immediately surrounded by many women. I'm the new toy, I assume.

"You got pretty teeth," says one woman whose teeth are rotted out from drugs.

"Um, thanks," I try to answer normally like the comment isn't completely abnormal.

Two other women take stools next to me. We begin the typical introductions. Most that surround us, I'm sure, are dying to hear why I'm here. I stick out like a sore thumb, and we all know it.

The woman to my left seems very young and immature, but she is the first to ask the question. "Hey, I'm Ashlyn. What brings you here?"

"A huge misunderstanding," I tell an abridged version and move on. They're probably disappointed with my answer, wanting to hear something a lot more dramatic like I killed my husband. "That's all of us, right? Misunderstood? What about you?" I ask her.

She laughs with her head back and looks at Laura and the other women at the table. My curiosity is piqued, this ought to be good.

"You've probably seen me on the news. I was charged with second-degree murder of a friend of mine. Oh, and my son was in the back of the car when it happened. Been here six months now."

I tell myself not to let my face react to what she's just said. My initial thought is how incredibly normal she talks and acts. Murderers are real people, after all. I remind myself that she's been charged, not convicted, and I don't know the whole story. I can at least offer her grace.

I can feel the intense stare from the woman across from

me. "What about you?" I ask, letting my eyes drift to hers.

"My *friend* accused me of breaking into her house and stealing some of her things." She starts cackling and grabs the table as she leans forward and vehemently says, "I needed the stuff in there! Half of it was mine, but she locked me out." The table erupts in laughter. They clearly have heard this story a time or two.

Her laughter trails off with a chuckle and a sigh, "I'm Helen, by the way."

"Nice to meet you, Helen," I say, laughing along with her.

Helen is in her 50s with salt and pepper hair that's tousled on top of her head and reminds me of a grandmother. Dark age spots speckle her sallow skin, and dark circles cover her dark eyes. Something seems to be lurking in her eyes. I hope to never find out what. She wears a back brace from a recent surgery that's left her in extreme pain, or that's what I'm told. I can't decide if she enjoys entertaining these women because she's bored or sadistic. Either way, it seems she has found an interest in me, and it puts me on edge.

Most of the women inmates are sitting around tables with tablets that Laura explains are to purchase things from the commissary and to text family members. All messages are monitored by the guards, so they use other means to communicate. Laura secretly tells me she has a way to speak with the men inmates here through the commissary app since they're not allowed to communicate. I'm not sure I want to be a part of the information she's about to share with me. So many social decisions are made instantly here. I listen as she describes intricately how their communication system works. Something about adding certain items into their shopping cart and the amount of that item represents a letter. Too confusing for me to keep up with, and quite frankly, I didn't pay much attention. I have no desire to secretly communicate with a male inmate here.

There are around sixty women in the room, and I see four telephones. Like a hawk, I watch as one becomes available, so I can call my mom.

"Hey baby, are you okay?" my mom answers.

"Yes, ma'am, I'm sorry it's taken me so long to call you. As soon as I got here, I was locked in an individual cell, and there are so many more women here vying for use of the phone. I'm lucky to have grabbed this one."

"Well, I already put money on your account so you can make phone calls to me as often as you need."

"Thank you, Momma."

"How is it there? I've been so worried about you."

"I know this sounds so strange, but it's way better here than at New Orleans City Jail. The people are so nice, even the guards are accommodating. So weird that I just said that."

I told her all about the female guard showing extra attention to me and about Laura and how normal she is. She sounds relieved by the time I'm done talking.

"Any word on when St. Charles Parish will come and pick you up?"

"The guards that booked me in said they were coming tomorrow. I can hardly believe it. Hopefully, this will continue to go fast. God's fingerprints are all over this, and I continue to give Him the glory."

"I'm so proud of you, sweetheart. Keep pushing through. You'll get there."

"I try not to think about Christmas, but I do hope I'm out by then, but it is only two days away. I need to keep my head level and the goal of getting out of here at the forefront."

"Well, I think I can sleep better tonight knowing you're emotionally stable and feel safe. I love you so much."

"I love you too. I'll call you in the morning."

When I hang up, I look around the room, and lo and behold. There hangs a clock. The sight nearly brings tears to my eyes. Something so simple that I take for granted. Not sure I'll ever look at a clock the same. This place is better!

"Hey Laura, can we go to bed at any time here?"

"Yeah, you can go lay down, just don't get under the

169

covers."

"Okay, I'm just so tired. Do you mind if I borrow that devotional you talked about earlier?"

"Sure! It's next to my bed."

After telling the other women goodnight, I make my bed on the top bunk and start reading and praying for what God has done. He has never left me.

16

My first thought when I wake is that it's Christmas Eve. If someone would've told me I'd be waking up in prison on Christmas Eve this year, I probably would've fainted. Never in my wildest dreams could I imagine myself here.

I slept so well last night, which probably had a lot to do with the Tylenol the nurse gave me for my headache. Ironically, I think the door being locked helped me sleep soundly. Knowing that a random person couldn't walk up to me without being woken by the opening of the door lulled me to sleep. The sun is barely up when breakfast is served. We form two lines as groggy bodies shuffle to get a tray. I survey the food, the same as New Orleans City Jail. Dry pancakes with no sugar or syrup, just plain batter. My stomach still can't handle this food, so again I give it away. Food is treated the same here, too, ravenous wolves eager to lap up my leftovers.

Laura has coffee from the commissary, and I'm given a used cup. We sit around the table drinking coffee and listening to stories of what we would be doing or should be doing instead of sitting here.

Ashlyn takes a seat next to me again. She has some papers she said she'd like to share with me. I happily oblige and try to make sense of what she's given me.

I casually mentioned last night that I'd like to join a non-profit for prison ministry or something similar. Now that I've seen the people within these walls, my heart aches for their reality and what it could be.

At the top of her page, she's written in blue ink the name of her charity.

"The non-profit would be to start a half-way house for women coming out of jail. To help them get back on their feet. Set them up with job interviews and daycare services if they have children."

I'm amazed at the thought she's put into this. Good for her, I think to myself. Then I realize she's trying to enlist my help since I'm a business owner.

"I think this is great, Ashlyn. You can tell your heart is in this. I'm proud of you, drawing this out wasn't easy to do."

"This is what I wanted to do before I got arrested. I still think I can do it. I just need to get these charges dropped and find a donor or business partner. You can take these papers if you want. I think if I get out, we can do this to-gether."

How can I even say no? She doesn't have much to hold onto in here.

"That sounds great Ashlyn, I'll try to keep up with you on the communication app, and we'll go from there, okay?"

"That sounds amazing!" She's genuinely excited and proud of herself. I want to keep my word to her, if she wants to see this through, and she's able to get out, I will help.

"Not to change the subject, but I read an amazing verse last night in the Bible Laura let me borrow. Do y'all mind if I share it with you?"

The nods of assent surround the table, and I head to grab Laura's Bible.

"Okay, let me find it here. It's Proverbs 20:22: "Do not say, 'I'll pay you back for this wrong!' Wait for the Lord, and he will avenge you."

"Wow, I'm going to write that down," Helen said as she quickly went to her room for a pen and paper.

When Helen came back, I asked if I could pray over everyone at the table. They all agreed, and we joined hands. The prayer resembled the one I prayed in New Orleans City Jail. I tried to go around the circle and pray specifically for each woman.

"Hey Laura, can you call my mom if St. Charles Parish comes to pick me up and let her know they've taken me?"

"I'd be glad to. Can you give me her number?"

173

"Yeah, do you have anything to write with? Her name is Gwen."

"Tribb, *Audrey*, please come to the speaker!" Comes a booming voice from the front of the room.

All eyes are following me as I jump and quickly walk to the guard control room speaker at the bottom of the tri-windows.

"Get your things. A St. Charles sheriff is here to transport you."

Mixed feelings are brought on again. Even though I've only spent less than twelve hours here, I've quickly bonded with these women and am unsure about what I'll face at the next stop.

Laura has already rolled up my mattress and is carrying it to me. She yells, "I love you," after me.

I'm too wrapped up in the chaos to say a formal good-bye to them.

"I'll keep up with you all!" I yell behind me, not wanting to make the sheriff wait and make my way to the now opening door.

After changing back into my old clothes, I wait on the waiting room benches meant for inmates. Two St. Charles Parish sheriffs are at the counter talking with the Jefferson Parish sheriffs. Their uniforms don't look like police uniforms, but more of a janitorial outfit. Boots, navy slacks, a light blue button-up loosely tucked in, and a wind jacket—a heavy-set woman with dead-locked face peers in my direction.

"Tribb?" she asks as if the mere mention of my name is a waste of her breath.

"Yes, ma'am."

"Get over here and keep your hands behind your back." She points to a spot in front of the padded wall.

Another round of being searched. Stubborn pockets still won't unbutton. St. Charles Parish may not have well-uniformed sheriffs, but they do take the process of handcuffing seriously. Not only are my hands and legs cuffed again, now a brown leather belt is being strapped around me so my hands can be bound to my waist and an image of prisoners from backwoods Louisiana settles in my mind from the 1920s. The reality hits me again—common criminal. At least my hands are cuffed in the front, so the ride to St. Charles Parish won't be totally uncomfortable.

Me and another inmate, a young man placed in the back, are put into a van much like the Jefferson one. I overhear the female St. Charles guard said we need to make a stop on the way to the St. Charles correctional facility.

Our driver, the other St. Charles sheriff, is tall, skinny, and pushing seventy-five years old. He's driving, so they put me behind him. He smokes nearly the whole way and apparently had a meal full of beans last night. No ventilation in the cab of the van coupled with cigarette smoke, his gas, and no air conditioner makes me want to puke. I keep my eyes focused out the window. They've put me in the only seat that is in the sun, but I dare not ask for the air to be turned on. The female guard made it clear that there wouldn't be any problems today and no talking, so I adhere to her advice.

Two more stops is all I can think—two more. I've made it through two. I can do this. After at least forty miles, we pull into what looks like a juvenile military boot camp. I wonder if we're dropping off or picking up.

The female guard gets out, and my question is answered as she opens the cab door and motions for the young man in the back to get out. The driver and I wait while they're inside. Why is Louisiana so hot in December?

Now's my chance, "Can you turn the air on?" I ask the old sheriff.

No answer. I wonder whether he can even hear me through the plexiglass.

"Can you turn the air on back here?" I say a lot louder.

"You wan' the air on?" he mumbles back.

"Yes, please, I would really appreciate it! I'm sitting in the sun!" I yell back.

He leans forward, puts the rear air on max, and immediately the cold breeze starts to hit my face. Smoke all you want to now, mister. I have cool air.

Half-relieved to be out of Chad's territory entirely, I'm still nervous about Mr. Emerson's parish. Does he also have strings to pull there?

"Sit here and wait," the heavy-set female guard tells me.

She hands my paperwork to the lady sitting at the booking desk—round three of being booked in. Instead of digital fingerprints, they take them in ink. Between the sheriff uniforms and the looks of the lobby, their budget must be low. Mugshot number three is taken, and I'm placed into a holding cell while they book me in. My body is beginning to ache from no food and barely any water. At Jefferson, you had to buy a cup, so I just didn't drink anything there. I can tell that I am severely dehydrated.

The holding cell is filthy. The only place to sit is on the bottom bunk. It has a mattress, but it's covered in crumbs, dust, and hair. For now, I choose not to sit. Instead, I squat against the wall. A square window on the door has been covered with a piece of cut plywood that the outside can raise to see in—no way to see out, other than a tiny slit in the side.

What feels like an eternity has passed. I knock on the door to ask for water. No answer. I let a few more minutes go by and knock a little harder. The plywood starts to move.

A young man who barely looks twenty-five lifts the makeshift cover. Unable to hear him, I attempt to read his lips.

"Yes?" he mouths.

"I need some water. Can I please have some water?" I say loudly, hoping he can hear me.

He gives me a thumbs-up, then lifts his finger and mouths, "One minute."

I nod my head and thank him.

My lips are so dry they're beginning to crack. The anticipation of water lifts my spirits for the moment. I keep waiting for the door to open, but the minutes seem to crawl. No one comes. The pressure on my knees is too much. Dirty mattress or not, it's somewhere to sit other than the floor. I try not to look as I sit on the edge of the mattress. Leaning my head on the metal bar, I close my eyes and wait. Dizziness overcomes me, and I start to worry that I'll pass out. The thought of water consumes me like a mirage.

Desperate and thirsty, I pound on the door with my fist. No one comes.

"I need water!" I shout, leaning on the door. Banging my fist again ignites a sense of panic in me. This is out of character for me, but I'm scared and terribly lonely.

"Please, I feel like I'm going to pass out!"

Bang, bang, bang! Someone in the holding cell next to me beats on our shared wall.

"What's up?" he shouts at me.

I don't want to get in trouble for talking to him, so I sit back down. My head is spinning. Chills rush over my body. Fever has set in. What I thought was a bad situation has just gotten worse. I'm sick with God knows what.

"Jesus, please put healing on my body. To be locked in this awful place with a fever will be unbearable. How will I get through this, God? Please don't abandon me!"

Resolutely, I stand up and head for the metal door again. I bang hard with my fist, "I need water!"

Feeling entirely helpless, I turn around and scan my cell. A dry toilet, sink that doesn't work, and the dirty metal bunk. This room is sealed shut. Flaxen yellow cement walls mock me that there's no getting out of this room, not on my own. The thought of laying down teases me, but my mind won't let my body near the nasty mattress.

Push through! Don't give up! I tell myself. I always used to tell people if you made your mind up to do something, you could do anything. I didn't consider if your body wasn't physically able to. I sit back down.

High ceilings add to the terrible echo as I whisper in a trance-like state that I need water. *Please, give me water. Please, give me water. Please, give me water.*

One last time, I tell myself as I stumble toward the brown metal door.

Bang, bang, bang, "Can I please have some water? I think I'm sick!" I wait and listen, silently urging them to come to the door.

The plywood cover is lifted. An older man this time faces me. He just stares.

"Can I please have some water?" I say as I make the motion of drinking.

He nods his head and drops the cover again. Oh, no, not this again. Sitting back on the mattress, I try to let go of the idea of water. Tears flood my shirt. I thought it couldn't get worse. I must've been begging for an hour for water. Why don't they let me have the smallest amount?

The door unlocks and opens. There stands the older man with a cold bottle of water. I race to him and grab the bottle.

"Thank you so much. I think I'm sick and running fever."

"No, you're not," he says plainly.

"Yes, sir, I know I am."

"No, you're not," he repeats.

Not knowing what else to say or do, I open the bottle and drink the whole thing without stopping. He left as soon as I started drinking. When I'm done, I sit back down on the bunk, aches and chills flood my body again. I try to rest my head on the metal bar and close my eyes.

I don't know how much time has passed since I got the water, but the door unlocks, and the same older man leads me to a locker room to change into my third set of prison wear, a light brown jumpsuit. They let me keep my shoes this time.

No phone calls have been allowed yet. I hope Laura called my mom to tell her, so Charles can bond me out of here and St. Tammany Parish can pick me up. I'm led back to the lobby, no cuffs, and told to sit in one of the waiting chairs.

"Your bondsman has already been here to place your bail," says the plump woman behind the desk.

Finally, a victory.

"I called St. Tammany to see when they are going to come pick you up because now we're just holding you for them," she continues.

"I'm sorry, Ms. Tribb, but they said they would come and get you after the holidays."

Tears run down my face, and sorrow permeates my soul.

"I called as soon as you posted bail, but they seemed reluctant to do anything because of Christmas."

"How long do I have to stay here?" I quietly ask.

"They have ten days to come pick you up," she uncomfortably says, her eyes betraying the guilt she feels. She doesn't want to break this news to me.

I take a deep breath trying to gather my thoughts.

"Thank you for trying," I tell her.

17

Christmas in jail. Is this really what they wanted? Are Ms. Broussard, Chad, and Mr. Emerson rejoicing that I'm here? Will this finally make them happy? I imagine them calling each other gleefully sharing in their news that I've been arrested and am not in my comfortable home surrounded by family like they are. I would never wish this on anyone, even them.

A gentle answer turns away wrath, but a harsh word stirs up anger.

In the beginning, when all this started to unfold, I chose to seek God's will. I prayed daily over this company before we ever started it. God was opening doors that only He could open. I still feel that I am walking in His will and what He wants for my life. When the accusations multiplied, I kept calm on the outside. Not reacting out of emotion like these clients did. I tried to maintain my composure like Jesus would've, knowing I was in the will of God. I still believe He has huge plans for me, plans I can't begin to comprehend. This is only part of the story, and it needs to be finished. I will see my way out of this.

With a crappy mattress in tow, they walk me to the female general population room. The layout reminds me of

New Orleans City Jail with bunks covering the room. There must be over seventy women in here and three toilets. Instead of telling me what bunk to go to, I'm allowed to choose. I half-wish they'd just tell me where to go. Quickly thinking, I head toward the back wall. A huge woman walks up to me and says I should choose the top of their bunk. With nothing to lose, I place my mattress and make my bed.

"I'm Priscilla, but everyone in here calls me 'Cissy,'" the vast woman tells me when I climb back down.

"Audrey," I meekly reply.

"Anybody bothas you in here, be shue ta lemme know," she bellows.

"Okay. Thanks." Weighing in at probably 225 pounds, I decide not to question her motives for now. She's well over six feet tall, and her accent leads me to believe she's from south of Houma. Her green eyes are serious, and her curly auburn hair sits in a bob.

"Why they pu' a lil' scrawny thin' like you in 'ere? What'd ya do, drugs?" she asks me seriously.

Again, I retell what happened. Her face reveals nothing.

Finally, she says, "Thas too bad."

"I got two kids, spanked the lil' one. My boyfrin's motha called the cops on me. Chile abuse, they say. I s'pose ta get out two months ago. Den, a girl, try ta steal muh food, so I popped 'er. Gave me anotha chahge."

I try to offer a feeble apology for what she's been through.

"Nah, I'll get out and git mah babies back, jus' gotta wait."

A few hours pass, no clock again. I called my mom as soon as a phone was free. I didn't want to talk long. Her voice reminds me of home and is a constant reminder that it's Christmas Eve. Supper came and went, bologna sandwiches—a step above what I've been served. At least I know what's in the bologna. I still feel incredibly weak and sick that I'm only able to eat half of the sandwich. My stomach can't take it. Cissy gladly takes it off my hands.

The speaker yells a garbled message, and a mass exodus of inmates begins leaving the room. Some stay behind. Unsure of what is happening, and no matter where they're going, I want to walk out that door. I follow along and find Cissy.

"Where are we going?" I whisper to her.

"Church. Christmas Eve service." My heart leaps, church!

We walk single file, but they haven't cuffed us. Even though I haven't been here that long, I enjoy being able to walk out of this room, uncuffed. The women pile into what looks like a cafeteria. Twinkling Christmas lights are hung above the serving line. My stomach drops, another reminder that I'm so far away from those I love. We get to choose where we sit, another freedom I count as a blessing. I take a seat next to Cissy.

A woman with wide hips and a shaved head walks to the front of the room carrying a Bible. Huh, an inmate is going to lead the service. She opens with a prayer. Everyone bows their head, and she begins to pray for protection, healing, and our families on the outside. I've never felt closer to God than right now in this jail service. These women are longing for God's forgiveness and love. It's palpable. He's right here in this room, comforting the hurt and loss.

She begins to sing, "Jesus Paid It All." Slowly, the voices around her join in as they hand out the lyrics.

I hear the Savior say

Thy strength indeed is small

Child of weakness watch and pray

Find in me thine all in all

Jesus paid it all, All to Him I owe

Sin had left a crimson stain

He washed it white as snow

Lord, now indeed I find

Thy power and thine alone

Came and changed the lepers spots

And it melt the heart of stone

Jesus paid it all,

All to Him I owe

Sin had left a crimson stain

He washed it white as snow

And when before the throne

I stand in him complete

Jesus died my soul to save

My lips shall still repeat

The echo of voices is almost ethereal. Singing each word emphatically, I let go and close my eyes. The tears overcome me. I'm torn. I feel so blessed to be in God's presence, even here. God knows no limits. These walls can't keep him out. What was meant to break me will be for good. His word promises me that, and that is what I cling to.

When we come to the verse, "melt the heart of stone," I can't help but think of Chad, Ms. Broussard, and Mr.

Emerson, and I'm struck with grief. What I thought would be difficult to do, came rather naturally. I prayed for them. Remembering that verse in Ezekiel: "I will give you a new heart and put a new spirit in you; I will remove from you your heart of stone and give you a heart of flesh." Lord, please give them a new heart. Not for me or my sake, but for theirs. Let them know the love You have for them.

After we sing, she begins her message. She speaks about making different decisions. That no matter what decisions we've made in the past, we can choose to move forward differently. Changed. We aren't defined by our decisions, even though it may feel like it. God is our judge at the end of it all. I soak up every word she has to say, not caring that it isn't traditional. I am so thankful for this moment in this journey, and I thank God for gifting me with this message.

When I think she's done, and we're to head back, two other women come forward and flank either side of her. She does an altar call. How amazing. About fifteen women head to the front, ready to pray and accept salvation. My heart soars. He's here, and I count myself privileged to have watched these women give their lives to Christ. Thank you, God! Even though this Christmas Eve wasn't traditional, it was still beautiful in its own way, and that doesn't escape me. My perspective instantly changes, and my hopes are lifted. I can decide to make this experience better.

Back in the general population room, the atmosphere

is buzzing. Everyone is happy, the TV is on, and there are groups of women playing cards. The spirit is catching, and I find myself next in line to play Spades. I've only ever played a few times.

My partner is a short, older woman, probably in her mid-50s, and full of energy. It's no secret why she's in here, seems to be all she talks about. Her husband was beating her, and she killed him.

"A resident of this fine establishment for seventeen years now. Murder in the first degree! He got what was coming to him!" she finishes with an eerie cackle. She doesn't deny it. Even sounds proud of herself. Everyone has their own demons to battle, in or out of jail. Cissy tells her to shut up and focus on playing cards.

The guards in St. Charles are much kinder than I anticipated. We have more freedom than any of the other places I've been in the last few days. They don't make us go to bed at 11:00, but you can if you want, and they leave the TV on. Curfew was extended to midnight tonight, probably because of Christmas Eve. It's warmer here too. I only use the blanket for comfort. Being on the third bunk nearest the ceiling helps me sleep more soundly. My hips ache from the various metal bunks I've laid on. I finally sleep.

My first thought when I wake is that it's Christmas day. The other jails were quick to move me on once I bailed out, not St. Tammany, Ms. Broussard's parish. Again, I wonder if

Ms. Broussard has anything to do with this. Small southern towns tend to have back alley agreements when it comes to things like this. All you need is a reputation and a handshake.

Only two of the three toilets work—two toilets for sixty women and no cleaning service. I haven't been able to use the bathroom for a week, shy bowels, I assume, coupled with not eating. Breakfast is what looks like should be oatmeal. Feeling feverish and weak, I lie back down. A few hours later, I get up and call my mom.

"How is it going there? Do you feel safe?" she asks, afraid to hear the answer.

"It's okay, not as clean as Jefferson, but everyone is nicer than at New Orleans City Jail."

We continue talking. I tell her about the Christmas Eve service and how incredible it was. She reluctantly tells me she's at my grandmother's house with the whole family. They've been praying for me and fully support me. There's the shame vine again, creeping to smother me. I'm supposed to be there, not here. What are they saying about me?

"Do we have any idea when they might come get me?" I ask her desperately.

"Honey, I'm not sure how to say this other than to just come right on out and say it."

I brace for the worst, not knowing what she's going to say.

"I did some research to see how long St. Charles could hold you before St. Tammany Parish could pick you up. It seems that they do have ten days, but those don't include weekends and holidays."

My legs nearly give out. I'm not sure what a heart attack feels like, but I fear my heart is going to explode out of my chest.

"Help me do the math on this, Momma, because I don't have a calendar. Today is Wednesday, December 25th."

"Right, and New Year's Day is a holiday as well, plus this upcoming weekend and next. That means the latest you'll have to wait is January 9th."

"No, no, no. Please don't tell me that. I can't do this. How is that legal? They don't count weekends and holidays, yet we're stuck in here for both?"

"They still may come tomorrow," she tries to offer.

"I know they're not." Rage sets in again then is quickly replaced by hopelessness. "I need to think. I'm going to lie down and pray."

My mind is still reeling from what she's told me. I have too many thoughts to process at once, and then simultaneously, I can't think. St. Tammany Parish and Ms. Broussard will be the death of me.

"Hey, you a'right?" Cissy stands at the side of my bunk.

"How is it legal that they don't count holidays and weekends when scheduling a transport? I'm not even an inmate here. St. Charles is holding me for St. Tammany. I've bonded out!"

"Listen, dere's not a thin' ya can do about 'dis right now. Sittin' up 'ere feelin' sorry for ya'self ain't gonna hep ya none."

She's not wrong. I climb down and join them at the table. I tune their conversation out as I continue to mull over possibly spending sixteen more days in here. I thought five days was a lot. St. Tammany Parish, who do I know besides Ms. Broussard that lives there and could help? Trying to find an angle, I rack my brain and come up with nothing. Might as well get used to the idea of two more weeks. My thoughts are interrupted as one of the other women at the table says we're having another church service tonight, except tonight will be a guest speaker. I find relief in this and relax a little. It's something to look forward to.

Weak and dehydrated, I lie back down. Seems that's all anyone chooses to do today. Sleep Christmas away. I can't help but to continue thinking about St. Tammany Parish. Why would they do this?

Several hours and two meals later, we head back to the cafeteria for the Christmas service. One of the sheriffs is standing at the front of the room. His cowboy hat and pressed pants make me nervous. Why is he here?

"Merry Christmas, ladies," his country twang begins. "I'm not technically allowed to do this, but I'm going to be givin' your sermon tonight."

A murmur goes around the room.

"Separation of church and state and all, but I figured this is a voluntary service, and you are choosing to be here rather than in general population. And quite frankly, I don't give a damn what my superiors say. God is my One and Only superior."

Applause and cheers erupt in the cafeteria. I can't help but to smile and enjoy every minute of this.

We don't sing this time, but the sheriff delivers an energetic and genuine sermon. Not preaching at us. He cares that we hear the Word today. His attitude is contagious, and we all leave in higher spirits than when we came in. Of all the guards, policemen, and sheriffs I've encountered in the last few days, the majority have treated me with respect and kindness. Just like the inmates, they are people under their uniform. Chad's position as a lieutenant police officer doesn't give him a blanket of immunity that he is a "good person." And not all inmates are "bad people." We're all just people, good, bad, and in-between, that have gotten caught up in our circumstances or emotions. Our split-second decisions determine our destiny.

Ms. Broussard, Chad, and Mr. Emerson chose to do this. They could have easily offered grace and gone about

it in a totally different way. Everyone suffers from the emotionally driven decisions they've made. They're still stuck
in a contract that I can't let them out of while I sit in jail.
Not sure they thought this through all the way. Regardless,
this is my current reality, and I have to continue finding my
way out.

18

St. Tammany doesn't come to get me for the next two days. Then it's the weekend. Sunday afternoon, I pray they will transport me tomorrow. My hopes aren't too high because Tuesday is New Year's Eve. I lie in bed, thinking how I'm going to survive this. "Lord, please help me. Give me comfort and peace that only You can provide." I've spent the last few days obsessing over St. Tammany Parish, trying to remember what towns are there and who I know that can help speed this process along. And out of nowhere, the thought drops in my head. Wait a minute, I can't believe I haven't connected the two yet. I race to the phone and call my mom.

"Hey, sweetheart, what's go—"

I don't let her finish, "Momma, I think I have a plan!"

"Okay...?" She sounds worried as she trails off. "You know these phone calls are recorded, right?"

For the first time in a long time, I allow myself to laugh.

"Yes, Momma. Listen, I need you to get in touch with Jackie's mom, Sonja. Jackie is a girl who's my age, but I hadn't even started on her project yet. Remember, they said they weren't going to press charges against me?"

"Yes, I vaguely remember you telling me that, but what does she have to do with anything?" She seems confused.

"She's from St. Tammany Parish! And from what Jackie's told me in the past, she knows everyone in town! Maybe she can call someone to go ahead and have me transported."

"Oh my goodness, this is amazing!" she shares in my excitement.

"Text or call Daddy and ask him to find her number in my phone, under Sonja. Call and tell her what's happened. I will call you back in an hour, okay?"

"Okay, I love you."

"You too. Pray this is the answer we need," I finish.

My anxiety is sky-high, and no amount of talking myself down from these high expectations is working.

The next hour seems to drag on. I keep asking people on the phone in my meerkat way what time it is. Finally, after fifty minutes have passed, I find a free phone.

"Well, did you get in touch with her?" I can barely get the words out of my mouth.

"Yes! She says of all people she knows the warden of St. Tammany jail!"

"WHAT?! That's amazing! Is she going to call him?"

"As soon as I told her everything that happened, she hung up with me and got him on the phone right away. She called me back and said they're going to pick you up tomorrow!"

"Praise Jesus!" I can't contain it, and I begin to sob. I can hardly believe what she's said. "Momma, thank you. Please somehow let Charles know, so he can meet me there tomorrow and bond me out. I don't want to stay there longer than I have to."

"I think your dad has already done so."

Sleep evades me as I imagine showering at home tomorrow and sleeping in my own bed. This is the last night on this painful metal bunk. It's almost over.

Monday morning, my spirits are high. This is the day I get to go home after a short field trip to St. Tammany. Looking back on all I've been through the last ten days, it's hard to believe I'm going home. They call my name around 10:00, dress into the clothes I put on all those days ago, searched again, hands and feet cuffed, and placed into a small, unmarked SUV. The female guard is friendly and lets me talk to her for the hour and a half ride to St. Tammany jail. Now and then, I get a glimpse of Lake Pontchartrain. I let my head lay back on the seat and let the sun hit my face. It's over. The hard part is over. Tears silently fall down my face.

The sign for St. Tammany jail comes into view, and it's nothing that I expected. It looks more like a shed. Tan and made of what appears to be tin, we pull into another sally port. As we walk into the building, I'm faced with a fifteen-foot-tall mesh gate. We wait to be buzzed through, and then I'm booked into the final jail. I hope that I don't have to undress again but am unsure if Charles even knows I'm here. Mugshot number four is taken, and I'm led to a bank of phones.

"Hey darlin', are you at St. Tammany?" my dad asks.

"Hi daddy, yes, I've just made it here. Is Charles on his way?" I ask, hopeful.

"I wasn't sure when they'd transport you. Let me call him and tell him you're there."

"Okay, I can't wait to see you. I need a good shower first," I give a small laugh.

"Let me call Charles and get you out of there, okay?"

"Alright, I love you."

"You, too," he says as he hangs up.

Now that I know Charles isn't on his way, I'm sure they'll have to place me in general population again. I try to remain upbeat.

Donning an orange and white striped jumpsuit, I'm cuffed and placed into general population. There's only around twenty-five women here, and it's cleaner than St. Charles. If only Ms. Broussard knew that Jackie's mom helped me be transported. She'd be livid, and for the time being, I relish in knowing she won't like it. Small victories are what keep me going. I have to remember to thank her when I get out.

"Hey, girl, what's up?" A loud and raspy voice says too close to me.

Shaken out of my thoughts, I see a rough-looking 5-foot nothing woman in front of me. She's mid-20s, and her arms brandish sores, no doubt from needles.

"Um, hi," I say quietly.

"What the heck are you in here for? You stick out like a sore thumb." She gives a hearty laugh.

"A misunderstanding." I won't be here long, and I don't feel like telling the story again. I'm weak, tired, and ready to go home.

"A quiet one, huh?" she says loudly.

"I just don't feel well, and I'm ready to go home."

"Go home? You're going home? You jus' got here!" She won't get out of my face. Just a bit longer, I tell myself.

"Yeah, my bondsman is on his way to get me out," I try to remain calm.

"Oh yeah? Well, thas good. Not me, I'm in here for a while," she emphasizes the last word with a chuckle. "Yep, I been caught too many times wit' dope. Then a guard tried to attack me, so I got 'im. They think they own you in here!" she screams to the one-way guard control room.

Please hurry up, Charles, I silently say to myself.

I arrived just in time for lunch: Bologna sandwiches and a sugary kid's drink. Cornbread and bologna sandwiches seem to be on the menu everywhere in Louisiana. This kid's drink is a first, though. Fruit punch, my least favorite, but I'll take what I can get. I drink it down, desperate for something to taste. Immediately I'm reminded of riding my bike around the neighborhood at eight years old. My life has turned out differently than I ever would've imagined. How can I be put in jail for something like this? That thought brings me to another, Sandy Colefield's words as she corrected me about going to jail, "You can be *arrested*."

"Tribb, Audrey," shouts the guard at the door. I hadn't even realized he was there.

This is it! I'm out!

Hoping this is the final time I put these dirty clothes

back on, I have half a thought to burn them when I get home.

For the first time, I see Charles. Tall, shiny bald head, looks like he's just come from the golf course in his slacks, white polo shirt, and ball cap. He shakes my hand.

"Nice to finally meet you, Ms. Tribb," he says with his southern drawl.

"You have no idea how good it is to meet you, Mr. Charles."

He double and triple checks that we have done our part so we can leave. He knows not to mess around with the legal system. I was hoping my dad would be here to greet me, but Charles offered to take me back home. Probably best that he doesn't see me or smell me like this. Charles opens my door, and we set off back to New Orleans, back to home.

We're halfway there when Charles' phone rings. The caller id says "Covington."

"Hmm, wonder what this is," he answers. "This is Charles."

Only hearing one side of the conversation, I worry after he says, "What? Ms. Tribb forgot to do what?" He looks over at me incredulously.

My heart is racing, what could have happened?

"She forgot to sign herself out? Okay, we're turning around. We'll be there in about fifteen minutes."

He hangs up and turns around. "Didn't I ask them several times whether we had everything taken care of?"

"Yes, I vividly remember that."

"Well, it's best to just get this taken care of. Otherwise, they'll come pick you up again."

My stomach lurches when he says this. He's right but going back right when I thought we were done dampens my spirits. A pit forms in my stomach.

On the ride back, we make small talk trying to find common ground. Eventually, we land on the topic of how I got myself into this mess. I told him about Chad being a police officer and the other clients. His reaction to my mention of Chad seems off. When I'm through telling him the story, he tells me how he was pulled into this and how he knows Allie.

"It was really weird because one of the police officers who picked me up at my dad's house said that Jefferson would be by for sure Saturday morning to transport me. Then they ended up not getting me until Monday."

He is quiet for a moment and then says, "The arresting

officer told you that?"

"Yeah, and then when I was being booked in, I over-heard the guards saying they wouldn't get me until Monday. At the time, I didn't question it. I know nothing about how all this works, so I trusted the system."

"My word." His statement hangs in the air.

"What?" I ask, wondering where he's going with this.

"I called Jefferson Parish Monday morning and asked why you hadn't been picked up yet. They said New Orleans City Jail never called them. Jefferson didn't even know you'd been picked up until I called them! At first, I thought it was just bad communication on New Orleans City's part, but now that you say this Chad character is a New Orleans City lieutenant, I can't help but put two and two together."

"Are you saying they purposely left me in there? That I could've been out on Saturday?"

"It's hard to believe anything else."

I try to process all of that. Lord, melt Chad's heart of stone and put one of flesh in him.

"Isn't that some form of police malfeasance?" I ask him.

"It's definitely false imprisonment. But you'd have to be able to prove that Chad instructed them not to contact Jefferson. You'll be hard-pressed to find a subordinate to turn against or even testify that their lieutenant told them to do something illegal."

"Right," I say. "And I'm the criminal."

19

Charles drops me off at home, no reason to be afraid to be here anymore. What used to be bustling with activity from my interior design company is now hollow and cold. Two huge glasses of water later, I'm standing in the shower. I stand there for half an hour, taking the time to let the hot water rinse away the last ten days. Bruises on my hips ache as I wash my legs. The metal from the bunks must've been worse than I imagined. When I pick my clothes up off the floor and head to the washer, the stench wafts to my nose. I couldn't smell how bad it was, poor Charles.

My dad suggested we go to dinner. I pop a couple of pills to ease my headache, put on a little mascara, and pull my wet hair in a bun. They brought all my stuff back home. It's like I never left. A hibachi grill restaurant will be the first place I eat a full meal in ten days.

Hunger left my body a long time ago. I feel what I imagine an animal feels like when they're being hunted—skittish and paranoid. My family is already seated when I walk in the restaurant. My dad makes his way for me as soon as he sees me. Wrapped in his bear hug, he holds me for a couple of minutes. It feels good to be held. I've missed human touch. The tears still don't come when I thought I'd be a basket case. I had played this scenario out thousands of times. What would my family say to me? What would they do? Next, my stepmom and brother walk over with smiles. They are glad to see me, and I to see them. We hug and then sit down.

The smell of food and grease doesn't stir my stomach for hunger but for nausea. As I watch the chef cook, I can't help but feel out of place. I remember this feeling and hate to be so acquainted with it. It's a reverse to that Friday night when they picked me up. I was taken from a warm, safe place surrounded by family and put in a cold, dangerous (to me) hell surrounded by strangers. Now I sit with very different feelings. I've lived through an experience that they can't even begin to relate to. I'm constantly wondering what they're thinking. Are they ashamed to sit with me? Do they blame me? Where would I even start to describe how I feel and what I've lived through the last ten days?

I sit and stare, picking up my fork out of routine and trying to appear normal and not emotionally removed, like none of this ever happened. But I can't pick up where I left off. I never will be able to. Life will be different now because of this experience. Do they want to talk about it? Or do they want me to be quiet? It's the biggest metaphorical elephant that I've ever been in the room with, and from what I can tell, my family wants to ignore it for now. All I want to do is talk about it, this life-changing experience I've just had. Maybe they think I don't want to. So I don't.

We veer to a safer topic. They have an upcoming trip to see my extended family. I choose not to go this year, even though they all know about what happened. I'm not ready for that yet. My mom is flying in to be with me. I'll be glad not to be alone.

"Why don't you stay at our house until your mom gets in town?" My dad asks after we finish dinner.

My initial reaction is resistant. I'm not sure I can handle being there so soon. The memories of that house aren't what they used to be. The thousands of memories made there were swallowed whole that night on the porch.

"I think it would be good for you to come back. To face it head on and not let our house be a scary place for you to visit." He says it like he can hear my thoughts. "Plus, I really don't want you being alone in your house when we're out of town." He, like me, is unsure if Chad will stop now that I've been punished and arrested.

He has a point. I agree, I don't want to be alone.

After a quick drive to my house to get clothes and an overnight bag, I make my way to my dad's neighborhood. My anxiety rises as I pull into their neighborhood. My car creeps around the corner, and their house pops into view. I stare at the porch, now without ferns. I imagine what I looked like surrounded by four police officers and a K-9 on the front lawn. The experience is surreal. I shake the thought away and park in the driveway.

My dad helps carry my bags back to the guest bedroom. Once he leaves and I'm left alone in the room, I stand there and replay that night. I laid on this spot on the floor and cried out to God, terrified. The feelings are so raw and real, but tears still don't come. Am I numb? Is this my body's way of dealing with all of this?

I hear the TV come on. Sports announcers are recapping the college football bowl games from today. I quietly shut the bedroom door. Where do I go from here? All that time spent sitting and thinking, I never really thought what I was going to do once I was out. My goal was just to get out. Thankfully, most everything will be closed for the next few days because of the holidays while I figure out what to do. What I *can* do.

My mom is flying in tomorrow night, and my dad and stepmom are leaving tomorrow morning. I'll be alone here most of the day. Part of me is worried, while another part needs quiet to plan out what my next steps are. Gathering what strength I have, I head to the living room to watch TV with my dad.

He's sitting in his recliner, remote in hand, just as I always imagine him. He gives me a slight smile, and I sit in the chair next to him. My stepmom comes in, and my dad mutes the TV.

"How are you doing, darlin'?" He's always called me that, now it really feels like home.

"I'm okay," I tread lightly here. I don't want to share all the gory details and make it worse for them or to cause them any more pain than they've already suffered at my hands.

"I'm sure it's going to be an adjustment," he continues.

"Yes, sir, dinner was awkward. I kept looking around, wondering who knew." The beginning of paranoia I had no idea would soon become worse.

"Oh, I did want to share a couple of interesting developments that I couldn't tell you on the phone. The detective who interviewed me while I was in Jefferson said he hated Chad."

"No way!" my stepmom says with a smile.

My dad doesn't really react, which I find odd. He's always been a man of few words, so I chalk it up to his personality.

Meanwhile, my stepmom has all the questions. I try to answer them as best I can. I recap the conversation the detective and I had and what brought on his very direct honesty. She seems genuinely intrigued. She's always been such an empathetic listener. I also share what Charles told me about Jefferson not even knowing I was picked up and that it most likely is false imprisonment. Again, no apparent reaction from my dad. I wonder what he's thinking. Does he believe me? Maybe it's helplessness.

After half an hour, we slip into silence. My dad says they have to get up early to get on the road, but for me to take the time and rest. I feel disconnected from him, and shame rises again.

Lying in bed, I toss and turn, not able to drift off as easily as I hoped or assumed. I'm consumed by terrible thoughts of what the future might hold for me. I refuse to check my social media. My mom had been routinely checking the local news, but so far, nothing had popped up. Who all knew about this stain on my name? I turned the TV on for the noise and distraction and finally fell asleep.

The sun is shining by the time I wake up. I didn't sleep as well as I imagined for the first night out of jail—more of my expectations falling short. The house sounds empty. I find a note on the kitchen counter with my dad's familiar, sharp handwriting:

"Feel free to everything in the fridge and pantry. There's Christmas ham. We love you."

Christmas ham, he knows that's my favorite. The first thing I want, though, is coffee. Now that my dad and step-mom are gone, I know I need to turn my cell phone on. I used Charles' last night to get in touch with my dad. I wasn't ready to face whatever my phone and messages held.

I turn the TV on again for company and more distraction. Holding my breath as my phone turns on, I wait for the notifications to begin coming in. Only three messages and a handful of voicemails. Almost everyone that I kept in daily contact with knew where I was. My email was the main thing I was worried about.

Opening my inbox, I scroll through the typical spam and eventually land on an email from Mr. Emerson, dated December 20, at 9:04, nearly thirty minutes after I was arrested. That can't be a coincidence. The subject is titled "Call me."

"Hey Audrey, I am worried about you. Hope your holidays are going well. Give me a call when you have a chance."

I can feel the blood reach my face. Is he taunting me? He filed criminal charges against me. He knows I was arrested. Is he serious, *hope your holidays are going well*? These people are making me question *my* sanity. He has some nerve, and I'm sure it's his guilt.

Quickly I type out, "As I'm sure you're aware, Mr. Emerson, I spent the holidays in jail."

I erase it and put my phone away. Now's not the time, and that is not how to do it. I need to speak with William first. There's something I've been wanting to do ever since I got here. Most would never want to look at the place again, but now that I'm here, I'm drawn to it. Opening the front door, I step out on the porch. For the moment, I re-live everything that happened, and finally, the tears come. Thoughts of embarrassment and shame. It happened, this is part of my life now. An open and bleeding wound. One day it will be a scar that I can't cover up or heal, but today it's an inflamed, aching wound. The kind that has a heartbeat. My heartbeat. Vulnerable and broken.

The world has new words for me. Fraud. Felon. Failure. Can I turn this around and replace those words? I can't, but I know my God can. He can replace those worldly words to Honest. Faithful. Redeemed. Restored. Loved. He promised me in His word that this life on earth would be tough, but with Him, I can do anything. Months ago, my stepmom reminded me that the Israelites wandered through the desert for hundreds of years trying to get into the will of God. Those were God's people, and He delivered them to the Promised Land. He didn't give it to them at first because their hearts weren't ready. They wouldn't have appreciated what God had given them. Most of the time, we think God is punishing us. Turns out he's waiting on *us*. My heart wasn't ready for the success I was about to have. I grew up in church and knew I was supposed to tithe my earn-ings and to seek God in everything. He just became part of my routine until He wasn't. I quit reading my Bible, and I wasn't praying. I've never felt closer to God than I did in those moments in jail when He was all I had. My life was shaken up, and my priorities were set straight again. Jail and isolation from the world have a funny way of making you realize what's important. My stepmom reminded me that God cares deeply for His people and when someone wrongs them, He will deliver them. In jail, I kept coming back to Psalm 32:7: "You are my hiding place; You will protect me from trouble and surround me with songs of deliverance." Songs of deliverance. I'm ready to sing, God.

20

Later in the day, I pack my things and head home to wait for Momma to get there. When I arrive, my house is silent. This is the longest I've been here since I was arrested. I keep all the curtains drawn and obsessively peek out of them every ten minutes. Are they coming for me? Will more charges be filed? I keep the lights and TV off, afraid of what I'm unsure. The worst has happened, but what could stop it from happening again? I don't have any more clients, but at this point, nothing would surprise me.

About an hour later, my mom pulls into the driveway, and I feel safe again, not being alone. We hug for what seems an eternity. It feels good to be held by my mom, who holds no judgment against me. She opens the curtains and begins to busy herself in the kitchen. My home is bustling now, alive. The people within a home are what make it one. It's New Year's Eve, and she says she's got a surprise for me. Not sure I can handle surprises right now, but I trust her, so I go along with it.

"I stopped at the store on my way here," she says.

"How did you manage that?"

"I used to live here. I think I can remember where the grocery store is. Oh, and the rental car has GPS, which helped."

We both chuckle.

"So, what are you making?" I ask her as I take a seat at the counter.

"Your favorite," she says in a sing-song voice.

"Etouffee?"

"Yes, ma'am, I found frozen crawfish at the store. Obviously, it's not as good as fresh, but it'll do for now."

"Is that the surprise?"

"No, we have a visitor coming," she says while she readies the stove with pots and pans.

My stomach flips. I don't want to see anyone.

"Okay..." I trail off.

"Don't worry, you'll be glad to see this person."

I can't think of anyone I'd be glad to see right now, but again she knows me best, so temporarily, I trust her.

She asks me to turn on the TV, so we can watch the ball drop later. Watching my mom in the kitchen puts me at ease. While she vigorously stirs her roux, we make small talk for now. How her flight was, how dinner with my dad went. We don't talk about the heavy stuff yet. I know we will. It's a rock sitting in my chest that I need to get out. I can't pretend and have life go right back to normal.

The doorbell rings. The blood leaves my legs, and my mom tells me to open the front door. Warily I open the door, and Laura is standing there.

"Sparklers, anyone?" she exclaims as she holds up a handful of fireworks.

Relief floods me, and she walks in to give me a hug. Laura has been there since the beginning, encouraging and praying for me. Our friendship has grown to heights I never imagined through this catastrophe.

"Come on, ladies, have some crackers and crab dip," my mom excitedly says. She was right, this was something I needed.

"When did you get in town?" I ask Laura.

"I've been at my parent's house since Christmas. Your mom has been keeping me in the loop about your release, so we both thought it would be good for me to be here to celebrate your coming home."

"Definitely a good surprise. Thank you for being here and for everything else you've done for me," I finish.

"Oh, Audrey, I can't imagine what you're going through. I just want to take your pain away. I want to fix it for you, and I know I can't, which is so frustrating for me."

"I know," I sigh, "we'll be on the road to recovery sooner than later, whether I'm ready or not."

"How do you feel?" she quietly asks me.

I take a minute to respond, gauging how I honestly feel.

"Tired mostly. And there's a feeling I can't explain. An emptiness or an inability to relate to other people now. Like I feel that I'm dirty and have been through an experience most people haven't. Most people I know anyway. I guess if you were to put a name to the feeling, it would be shame."

"Sweetheart, please don't be ashamed. You're entitled to feelings, but not that one. This isn't on you," my mom says gently.

"Part of me believes it is. *They* didn't go to jail. I was the one sitting in those jail cells with prisoners. I was a prisoner." The thought even now consumes me. It's something my brain physically cannot process, and I don't even know where to start to process it. My brain is resisting the whole thing. I want to wake up tomorrow and none of this ever happened. Tears come again. They wrap me in a hug.

Laura begins to pray, "Dear God, we ask that you fill sweet Audrey with peace and understanding, Lord. We don't know why this happened, God, but we know You are the creator of the universe and are not taken by surprise. Please fill us with Your love. Help Audrey to pick up the pieces and guide her on her new journey now. We know that You have placed her on a new path. Help us to trust Your sovereign plan, God. Most of all, Lord, we ask for

Your healing. Put emotional healing in Audrey's body. She needs Your love God more than ever. We thank You for what You've already done, God, and we ask this in Your most heavenly name. Amen."

We break apart, and I instantly feel lighter. Laura was able to speak directly to my needs. She was my advocate. All this time, I felt that's what I needed, someone to speak for me when I couldn't. I truly never thought it would get this far, so I didn't fight it like I probably should've. When the arrest warrants came out, it was like I was living in a fog. And denial. People are forgiving and gracious, they wouldn't purposely try to hurt me for an honest mistake. My heart breaks. Yes, they would.

After supper, we sit in the living room. My mom cozies up on the couch while I'm in my favorite recliner and Laura's in the chair next to me. Home. Momma lit the fireplace, and noise from the New Year's program can faintly be heard in the background. Eleven days didn't seem long before, but it was an eternity in there. Will there ever be a day I don't think of this? Can I escape my present reality?

Momma is the first to break the silence, "Audrey, do you want to talk about what the future might look like?"

"Yeah, we need to. I need feedback," I say as I stare at the crowds on the TV trying to get their two seconds of fame. This is just another New Year's for them. It's so different for me. None of them just got out of jail.

"You have tomorrow as well to figure out what your next steps will be, but Thursday everyone goes back to work," Momma finishes.

"I guess my first step is to schedule a meeting with William."

"What about Chad? Are you going to file a complaint with the Department of Justice that he chased you in his police car without probable cause and had you falsely imprisoned?" Momma asks. She's most angry at Chad. I guess I would be, too, if it happened to someone I love.

"My gut reaction is, yes, to definitely file a complaint against him. Why am I held to a higher standard than he is? I just need to talk with William before I make any concrete decisions."

"So now do you have to go to trial for each of these cases?" Laura says quietly.

I take a deep breath, "My greatest fear is going to trial. I could be in jail for much longer if they found me guilty, years, I'm sure. I don't know if I'm willing to run the risk of that. Just cut my losses and move on, you know?"

"Are you sure, honey? I mean, they went after you with all they had, it might end differently than you think. They just get off scot-free? No one is held accountable for what they did?"

"I'm not sure I have any fight left after all this, Momma. My main thought has been to return kindness. I want to be a living testimony. I want to offer grace when they didn't. Most of all, I want to pray about each decision going forward. Sometimes I'm caught somewhere between turning the other cheek and not being a doormat. To set an example that not anyone can do this to me again, but overwhelmingly I feel to offer grace. I can't explain it. I just feel that's what I'm supposed to do."

The room is silent for a few minutes.

Finally, Laura begins, "Ultimately, Audrey, it's definitely your decision. But I'm with your mom on this one, at least talk to William before making any final decisions. See what your options are. It says in your contract that your clients are not to communicate, and we all know it would be easy to find proof that they did just that, broke the contract, and that's just the beginning."

"You're both right. I just keep playing out in my mind that no matter what, black and white, the license was wrong. There's no getting around that. Is that a risk I'm willing to go to court for? To risk my freedom for? Do I want to be talking about this one or two years from now? I'm not sure anymore. I'm just not sure."

We hear the TV announce, "twenty seconds until the start of the new year."

"Let's get the sparklers and go outside," Momma says as she jumps up to grab the lighter.

Laura and I follow suit and head for the backyard. We leave the door open, so we can hear the countdown. My mom lights our sparklers, and we sing the familiar New Year's Eve rendition of "Auld Lang Syne."

"Should old acquaintance be forgot,

And never brought to mind?

Should old acquaintance be forgot,

And auld lang syne?

For auld lang syne,

My dear, for auld lang syne,

We'll take a cup of kindness yet, for auld lang syne."

Right here in this brand-new year, on this brand-new day, these lyrics don't escape me. Before the song confused me, now everything has new meaning, even this ambiguous song. New year means new beginnings. That's what I've always been told. Hopefully, this metaphor will predate itself.

"6, 5, 4, 3, 2, 1, Happy New Year!"

Fireworks across the neighborhood begin to erupt. We all hug and welcome the new year with open arms. Two days ago, I couldn't imagine being this at peace, but a sense of dread begins to rise, and I know this fight isn't over.

21

Momma, Laura, and I spend New Year's day lying around, eating, and talking. When they're not looking, I find myself peeking out the windows. Waiting, again for what I'm not sure. Around 2:00, my phone dings a text message.

"When are you going to finish my project? You better answer me, or don't think I won't file more charges against you."

I nearly collapse. Mr. Emerson. At least Chad has left me alone in the way of communicating with me. Mr. Emerson, on the other hand, is relentless.

"Who's that, Audrey?" Momma asks.

I show her my phone. She gasps.

"What's going on?" Laura says as she makes her way over to us.

I hear my mom reading Laura the text message. I knew my happiness was short-lived. I forgot who I was dealing with.

"Audrey?" Laura's voice breaks into my thoughts.

I shake my head as if the action will scatter the contents inside, "Yeah?"

"Why don't you email William and ask when you can

meet with him? We have to get ahead of this, this time."

"Yeah, you're right," I almost whisper.

"I'll do it," Momma says as she taps on my phone. "William, I got out of jail on Monday. Mr. Emerson is already harassing me today. We need to meet this week to talk about what I need to do to resolve all of this."

"Take out 'harassing.' Say, 'contacted me regarding his project' instead."

"Okay." She goes back to the phone and finishes, "Sent. Well, that's done. Why don't you lay down and rest, Audrey?" She must've seen the exhaustion I felt.

"That sounds like a good idea. Laura, do you mind?"

"Not at all." She stayed the night last night since the drive to her parent's house is at least forty-five minutes. We didn't want her on the roads that late, especially on New Year's Eve. We talked until the early morning hours of New Year's Day. Rest was exactly what I needed.

I left my phone in the living room for my mom to monitor in case William emailed back.

When I wake, the light from the windows reflects what looks like evening. I hear Momma and Laura laughing in the other room. For the moment, I'm relieved to have them here. I felt safe while I slept.

"Hey, sleepyhead," Momma notices me as I walk into the kitchen.

"I didn't mean to sleep that long," I say mid-yawn. "What time is it?"

"5:15," Momma answers with a small laugh.

"What's funny?"

"I just remember how many times in the last eleven days you've asked me what time it is. I've never looked at the clock that much in my entire life!" I can't help but laugh with her. Seems I wasn't the only one who found that funny. I guess humor can be found in any situation. It's all about perspective.

"William emailed while you were asleep. Asked if tomorrow at 1:00 was okay."

"Oh good, did you email him back?"

"I didn't want to overstep my boundaries. Thought I'd let you do that."

"Okay, thank you."

Quickly, I type a response confirming the appointment with William. I copied Allie on the email, so she'd be there too.

Laura's going back to her parents tomorrow, so the rest of the evening is quiet and relaxed while I mentally prepare for what tomorrow might bring.

Allie meets me at William's office. My mom stayed at my house; I didn't want to get her more involved than she already is. This is my burden to bear. Plus, she agreed to make our favorite Mexican dish, Carne Adovada.

"Hey, you," Allie half-runs to me. "You're a sight for sore eyes. How are you?"

"I'm okay," I say as we hug. "How are you holding up?"

"Well, I didn't spend Christmas in jail, so I guess I'm good. I *hate* that this happened."

We walk together out of the parking garage and up to William's office. I grab some candy from the candy dish as soon as we step in. My anxiety needs something to focus on other than the thoughts running rampant in my head.

The receptionist greets us from her desk, "Hi, ladies. Y'all here to see Mr. Stewart?"

"Yes, ma'am," Allie answers.

We take a seat in the waiting room. We barely get comfortable before William comes down the hall.

"Allie, Audrey, y'all come into the conference room."

I can't help but remember the last time I sat here a few months ago with Mr. Westwood, lightheartedly talking about a very dark future for me. Now, William takes the head of the rectangular table while Allie and I sit together to his left. The windows overlook the city. I've always thought New Orleans looked different from this view. Serene.

"You've had a tough couple of weeks, Audrey. I got the email from your dad, but there wasn't anything I could do as far as getting you out," he begins.

"I know. I'm just glad to be out."

He regales a time when he was arrested and had to spend some time in jail when he was younger. I'm only half-listening. He's trying his best to relate to me.

"Where should we start first? You mentioned in your email that Mr. Emerson in St. Charles Parish contacted you yesterday?"

"Yeah, he said he'd file more charges if I didn't begin work on his project. I guess I legally can now since the license is correct. I don't want to talk to him, though. From what I can gather, he doesn't have an attorney, which means we'll have to deal with him directly. I'd like to finish the project from a distance. I can send whomever out there, but I'd be suited just fine never seeing or hearing from him again."

Allie speaks up, "I can take over for the Emerson project."

"That would be great, Allie. I will reach out to Mr. Emerson and ask if that's all he requires. We need to do whatever it takes to keep him calm. He sounds like he could go off half-cocked at any moment. Also, I'd like to get him to agree not to press any further charges. Then work can resume. I can't have you in such a vulnerable position again," William finishes.

The thought of him protecting me makes me relax. I realize this is just a job for him, but to me, it's everything.

He takes a deep breath and rustles the papers in front of him, "Okay, now onto Mr. Ewing."

Ugh. I retell what Charles told me about New Orleans City jail not calling Jefferson and how that might be Chad's doing.

"Your bondsman is right. Proving Mr. Ewing conspired with fellow police officers to keep you in there will be difficult. They have a 'blue code of silence.' However, I still want to get the settlement finalized before we try to go after him."

"Blue code of silence?"

"Essentially, it's that they won't turn each other in for breaking the law. It's very fraternal."

I have no words for this. That sounds like a different battle for a different day.

"But there are charges that I can file against him for his inappropriate use of his badge?"

He scoffs, "Absolutely, there're tons under police misconduct."

"I guess we'll make that decision when the time comes."

William waits a beat, then continues, "I'll email Chad's attorney and move forward with signing the settlement documents."

"Have you heard from Ms. Broussard's attorney?" Allie asks him.

"Actually, yes, a few days ago, her attorney emailed me. Said Ms. Broussard wanted to retract her original settlement offer of $35,000."

The hits just keep on coming. She thought she'd strike while I was vulnerable and sitting in jail. She's not wrong that I'm desperate to get this over with.

I hear Allie sigh, "Okay, let's hear it."

I brace for his response.

"$18,000."

The air left the room.

"That's $17,000 less than we agreed on!" Allie furiously spits.

"I know," William relents.

"Do it."

Allie turns to me, "Audrey?! We can't let her do this to you and then get away with our money!"

"Are you sure, Audrey? You don't even want to counter?" William asks me seriously.

"Allie, listen, I never want to go back there. Ms. Broussard knows it, but at this point, she has the upper hand. We don't have any room to bargain. I guarantee that's all the money she has. She doesn't have the money to pay us back."

The distant sound of talking can be heard outside the room. William is patiently waiting on our final response.

"I'm not willing to gamble a trial. I don't have the money to pay William as it is, sorry, but I don't."

"You don't have to apologize, Audrey. Civil litigation is the costliest thing as far as court costs go. My advice, sadly, would be to settle and get this thing out of your way, Allie. I know that's not what you want to hear, but I agree with Audrey on this. I've been to trial more times than I can count. The majority of the time, it never goes the way you imagine. It doesn't matter what injustice you feel, you have to remember the other side is fighting for their cause too. No holds barred. Not only will money be lost, but this could drag on for years, and in the end, you still may not get the full amount. Plus, the license, which is the premise of this disagreement, is wrong, and that puts you immediately most likely losing," William says as he flips his pen in his hand.

Allie is chewing the inside of her cheek, obviously mulling over what the right decision is.

"Fine, settle with her. I'm already tired of hearing her name. I guess I don't want to be even thinking about her a year from now. She can get on with her sad, miserable life and call this her victory. I don't doubt for a second that what you put out into the world doesn't come back ten-fold to you, though. Here's hoping Ms. Broussard is buckled and ready for whatever life will throw at her."

"Nobody wins here, Allie," I say, trying to diffuse her anger.

"She does. Right now. You can't tell me that she's not going to tell everyone she knows that she won and how we mistreated *her!*"

"The truth will come out, I feel that it will, but we won't be the ones to do it," I put my hand on her shoulder and wish I didn't feel all the anger that she does. We're not running scared anymore.

"I have one more person I'd like to talk about," I turn back to William.

"Okay?" He seems visibly confused. Those are all the clients we have issues with.

"Sandy Colefield, the compliance investigator with the state. She walked Ms. Broussard through every step on how to criminally charge us. However, the Board continues to stand by their statement that they don't press charges against designers."

"I've been thinking about this. The only problem I see off-hand is that she's with the Board. Do you want to be an enemy of the Interior Design Board in the state you work in? That's a big enemy to have."

"They've never been our ally, not through this whole thing. I consider them an enemy now. We went to them for help, and they basically threw up their hands and said they couldn't. Sandy Colefield is one of their own, like Chad. Their *people* protect them. Meanwhile, we're hung out to dry."

"I still think we should get these cases settled and then determine what our next steps are," he finishes.

Part of me wants to take his advice, while the other part wishes we could release hellfire and brimstone on them all.

22

As promised, Momma had Carne Adovada ready when Allie and I arrived back home. We sat over dinner and told her about our meeting with William.

"Why did Ms. Broussard lower the settlement amount by so much? And how can she do that after y'all have already reached an agreement?"

"Your guess is as good as mine, but we hadn't signed anything to make it legal yet, so I guess she can do anything," Allie replies.

"She didn't have the money. She never did. That's what this whole thing is about at the end of the day. Money. Who has it and who wants it."

"What about the other ones? Chad and the one in St. Charles Parish?" Momma asks.

"We're going to finish Mr. Emerson's project and settle with Chad," Allie tells her.

No one is sure what to say, so we eat in silence. Any silence is deafening anymore, but not in the way you'd think. It's the unwanted guest that brings dangerous thoughts and words. My recent favorite, *felon*, that rushes in when it's quiet. The word won't leave me alone. It feels like a giant dirty secret, some misdeed. In reality, that's exactly what it is. At war again, I'm reminded of how ludicrous this all is. I try to put myself in their shoes. Would I have filed criminal charges against someone for this? If I didn't have the money to pay them, like Ms. Broussard. Still, probably not, I'm not that bold. Turn the other cheek or go after them with everything I have? I try to look at the real reason I want to turn the other cheek. I'm scared. When I accidentally wronged them, I was arrested and jailed. I have a hard time imagining what they'd do if I tried to harm them on purpose. I'm unnerved and want it all behind me. This isn't a battle I'm willing to even entertain.

Momma left two weeks ago. It's been eerily calm. I never understood that phrase, "calm before the storm." It's never calm before a storm. The winds are foreboding and warning of the storm's arrival. Distant lightning and thunder tell that it's on its way. No, the calm is in the after when the damage is done, and you're left to survey what's left. That's when it's quiet and serene.

No one calls any more demanding answers. The damage has been done. Surprisingly, the story hasn't been on the news, and my social media accounts have been left alone. Either people know and are giving me privacy, or since I'm not brandishing any success, they've left me alone. It's like it never happened. Did it happen? I have attorney fees and a mountain of debt that say so. I put my house up for sale. I need the equity and a new address. The pain is still here, my only visitor lately.

Allie is nearly finished with Mr. Emerson's project. He agreed to drop the charges once it's complete. I hope he follows through. I've only recently discovered who he really is. Although he revealed just a glimpse when he filed charges, I had no idea what he was capable of until last week.

On my way to a doctor's appointment, my phone rang, and the caller id revealed Mr. Emerson's name. Reacting without thinking, I hit the answer button.

"Hi, Mr. Emerson," I quickly said.

No response.

"Mr. Emerson?"

From my car speaker, I hear muffled voices.

"Hello? Mr. Emerson? Did you mean to call me?"

The voices sound far away, but I think I can make out Mr. Emerson's. I pull into the nearest empty parking lot, straining to hear what's being said. There are pros and cons to having a name at the beginning of the alphabet and phone book. People always accidentally call me. This time, though, it's a pro.

"I kept her there through Christmas," Mr. Emerson sounds closest to the phone.

They're talking about me. Who could he be talking to? I still can't figure out who the other voice is. It's too far away.

"Yeah, Chad and I went together on this. He's a New Orleans cop. You could say we didn't have much standing in our way to get her."

I grab my mouth, trying to stifle what I've just heard. Fumbling for my phone, I press record.

For the next twenty minutes, Mr. Emerson practically lays out how they did it. Chad's warrant was stagnant in Jefferson Parish. They needed a new one to be able to "visit" me again to try to pick me up. All it took was a phone call from Chad to give Mr. Emerson a slight nudge convincing him to file an arrest warrant for the same charges Chad filed. There's that herd mentality. Mr. Emerson filed on Tuesday, the arrest warrant was served that Friday. Four days. That seems unheard-of. From what I've read, this is extremely rare. In fact, even violent criminals get more time than that, months even. Months. The only way to serve one that fast is to have wronged someone on the inside. My blood begins to boil. Chad has abused the system and has the gall to call me a criminal. What's that saying? Those who live in glass houses shouldn't throw stones.

When Mr. Emerson is finished proudly telling his story,

I hear the phone come closer to his voice. It hangs up. He's just realized I've been listening. What I wouldn't give to see the look on his face.

I call him back. Surely, he's seen how long I was listening. He doesn't answer but instead sends a text.

It reads: "Hi Audrey, do you mind if I call you later?"

Caught red-handed. He's going to try to get his story straight, I assume. It's sure to be a good one.

I reply: "Sure. Look forward to speaking with you."

Riding on the wave of my newfound confidence, I forward the recording to Allie and William, and I wait.

Later that evening, I begin to wonder whether Mr. Emerson will call at all. I finally have collateral to getting these charges dropped against me, and the thought exhilarates me.

I jump at the sound of my phone. Mr. Emerson.

"Hello?" I answer.

He sounds wary, "Hi Audrey. How are you?"

"Hey there, Mr. Emerson. I'm doing okay, how about you? It's been a while since we've talked."

He pauses, "Yeah, Allie's doing a great job. We're almost finished."

"So she tells me." We're both tiptoeing around the topic he doesn't want to discuss, and I'm dying to dig into.

I don't wait for him to bring it up, "Did you have a good talk earlier?"

"Listen, Audrey. I meant for you to hear all that. I knew you were listening."

The absolute nerve of this guy. I didn't think he could shock me anymore, and yet here I am again in disbelief.

"Right. All that was planned out?" Does he know I'm not buying this?

"Yeah, I wanted you to know," he says nonchalantly.

"That doesn't make sense. Why would you tell me all the laws you and Chad broke?"

"I was trying to let you know about Chad and his role in all of this."

"Then why wouldn't you just tell me?" I can see where this is going. He's the weak link. The one who would turn on you if you got arrested. The squealer. He'd be the first to get a plea deal. Wonder what Chad would say if he knew. He can bargain with himself all he wants, that he's doing the right thing, but I know better. He's saving himself.

"Are you going to drop these charges, Mr. Emerson?"

The question hangs in mid-air.

Finally, he answers bluntly, "I've already said that I would."

"When? I want to know a date."

"As soon as our business together is through."

I don't let him know that I recorded him. I'll let him wonder nervously, never knowing.

23

It's March. Three months have passed since that phone call with Mr. Emerson. William said to hold onto the recording. That we could use it as collateral if he didn't drop the charges. It always seems that I have all this evidence and William's answer is always, "Let's get this settled first."

Allie and I signed settlements with Ms. Broussard and Chad. What we've waited months for seemed completely underwhelming. There were no celebrations. We felt we couldn't really celebrate until all the charges were dropped. Here we are three months later, and all charges remain, save Ms. Broussard's St. Tammany Parish. They were the quickest to reach out and order me to pay $1,200 to have the charges dropped and my record expunged. Money. This is a business, not a legal system.

Chad sent a request to the Jefferson District Attorney for the charges to be dropped. Who knows if this is just a formality, and they've got some sort of back door handshake agreeing they'll pursue us. I heard through the grapevine that Chad's attorney's husband was a Jefferson Parish ADA. William says I have nothing to worry about, but I don't know what to believe anymore.

Mr. Emerson's project is complete. I still haven't visited his house since the week of my arrest. From what I can tell through pictures Allie has taken, we did a beautiful job. Mr. Emerson keeps assuring us that he's contacted the Assistant District Attorney for St. Charles Parish, but we've heard nothing. I don't believe him.

They were all so quick to file these charges. It's amazing how fast they were able to do it. Now we can't get anyone to move on our behalf. I'm reminded that the Lord is just, and He is all we need. I know He's working in the midst of this, and one day I'll be able to see His fingerprints all around.

I've slowly told my closest friends what happened. Each of them offered full support and wished I would've told them sooner, so they could've been there for me. It's tough to explain why I didn't. How can I even describe the shame I'm *still* plagued with? I vividly imagine myself standing over a tombstone labeled "Audrey's Pride" with a deceased date of that fateful day in December. Rising from the ashes is the three-headed monster named Shame. No one can understand how deep this wound goes.

My dad said I should start going back to church, that it would only help. He was right. It felt so good to be back in God's presence when a few short months ago, that's all I wanted.

Allie and I put the company on hold. I'm not ready to

dive back into work. She's ready and has new clients ready to sign contracts. More and more, I've started to question whether this is what I'm supposed to do, interior design. The risks of owning a business have outweighed the rewards. We haven't seen any since we began Magnolia Maison. Just heartache and turmoil. What I want to do is use my talents for God. But how can I do that? My pastor preached a message a couple of weeks ago about using your natural gifts for the kingdom of God.

"Take something that you like to do," he says with his left fist, "and something that you're good at," looks to his right fist, "and find your purpose there," he says, bringing his fists together.

Boom, it hit me right in the chest as if he punched me with those fists. Granted, this wasn't Moliere material, but still profound. I just went with interior design because it seemed interesting, and that's what girls my age were doing at the time. Get a degree and get a job is what I was always told. Just a perk if you enjoy doing it too. I like interior design, but does it drive me to get up every morning? No, especially not now.

Over the course of the last six months, my view has changed when it came to two things: People who can't afford bonds while stuck in jail in a broken system and those who have no understanding of the legal system, especially interior designers. This couldn't happen again to someone. The Interior Design Board is not an advocate for interior designers. We need an advocate. After all, make your mess your message. What a mess this was. And as Moliere *does* say, "The greater the obstacle, the more glory in overcoming it."

After that church service, it was like a switch clicked on inside of me. This was it. I finally realized why I went through this. As soon as I got home, I took to writing my plans. In the quiet of my kitchen, my brain was on fire, scribbling down all the ideas that came flooding in. I called Allie and told her to come over right away.

"What's going on, Audrey? I have to admit this is the most animated I've seen you in months. Is everything okay? Did you hear something from William?" She seems frantic, more curious than anything.

"Sit down and bear with me."

"Okay..." She draws it out and slowly sits in the chair across from me. She's unsure what I'm going to say.

"I want you to take over Magnolia Maison completely."

Before I'm even finished, she interrupts, slamming her

purse on the table, "No! I would never do that to you. This is your baby. Your company."

"Not anymore. I want to do something different. I have a whole list of ideas."

"Like what?" She sounds breathless and stunned.

"How did we get into this mess? No one helped us to create a business or check to ensure the license was correct."

"Right, but how could we have changed that?"

"College. Yeah, they prepared us to go to work for someone else, but actually owning a business? No one helped or even guided us with that. I'm going straight to the universities. I'm going to petition that they have law courses added, so right out of the gate, they know the law, not learn it on the back end like we did. They need to better equip them for starting a business."

"But universities take forever to do anything, especially when it comes to their curriculum."

"I don't care how long it takes. This can't happen again. After I'm done with the universities, I'm headed for the licensing board. I might even create my own union!"

"Aren't you getting ahead of yourself?"

"No, I haven't seen more clearly than I do right now. As hard as it was for us to go through this, there needs to be a purpose. We can't let this go by the wayside and not fix the system. You have to admit that what they did to us was overkill."

She looks down at the table and absentmindedly rubs the tablecloth between her fingers. I know the guilt she's been battling because it was her license.

"Listen, Allie, do you agree that we can't let this happen to anyone else?"

"Definitely."

"Okay! I'm not even done telling you the rest!"

She laughs, "It is good to see you passionate again."

I lower my voice, "I'm going to change the law."

"Hmph, yeah, right."

"No, I'm serious. A felony? For a license? Maybe for someone practicing without a license, but we had one, just the *wrong* one. That at least should be a misdemeanor! We're not doctors operating without a license. We are interior designers, for crying out loud! Our *crime*, if you can even call it that, wasn't drug-related or violent. If that was the case, why did they just hand us the correct license with us not having to take a test? We paid the application fee, and bang, we're granted it. The system is obviously flawed."

"You're not kidding. I love your energy. I'm just afraid

this will take you longer than you think. At least keep a portion of the company for income. It'll look better when you go speak to all these people that you're still being affected by the law directly."

"You'd let me do that?"

"Audrey, we've been through so much together in the last year, and a lot of it was because of my license. This is the only way I can pay you back for everything."

I reach over and give her hand a squeeze.

"One last thing," I quickly change gears.

"Oh no, there's more?" she laughs, and I do too. The energy in the room is palpable and alive again.

"Yes, but this isn't interior design related. When I was in jail, there were so many people just sitting and waiting. Their bail had been set, but no money to pay it—measly amounts less than $500. I want to connect with a non-profit to pay someone's bond once a month. I'd make sure they were non-violent crimes and have them send me a list under $500. Most people in there were for unpaid traffic tickets. Can you believe that?"

"Good for you Audrey, I think I will do that too. When you get the information, pass it along to me, okay?"

"Absolutely!"

"Okay, I think that's it," I say as I sit back and gauge

Allie's face.

"You better get started. You have a lot of work cut out for you. I'm proud of you," she says quietly.

24

A couple of weeks go by, and life generally goes back to normal—my new normal. I've begun research on the curriculum change at the university level. They've agreed to meet with me next week. That's at least a step in the right direction. I found a non-profit that helps prisoners post bail and set up an account with them to take care of someone once a month. There are some days I don't even think about my time in jail, but I know there are still people sitting in there, waiting.

Finally got the charges dropped and my record expunged in St. Tammany Parish, Ms. Broussard's chapter is finally closed. One down, two more still to go. Mr. Emerson has requested St. Charles' District Attorney drop the charges. I was shocked that he did what he said he'd do. He's either driven by guilt, or he knows I have proof. Now I wait to hear what their terms are. Again, I'm sure it revolves around money.

A week later, St. Charles Parish mailed me a letter saying they were dropping the charges, but again I'd be fined. This time it was only $500. Another one down. The irony doesn't escape me that both "Saint" parishes are dropped, St. Charles and St. Tammany. Now just Jefferson Parish left. Still waiting on my July court date next week. The thought is never out of my mind, and as the date creeps closer and closer with each day, my anxiety rises higher and higher. Will I have to face Chad? William said they most likely wouldn't drop the charges until our day in court. Looks like we'll have to play the wait-and-see game and play a part in the theatrics. I keep reminding myself that God is in control, not Audrey.

My day in court has finally arrived. I worry Chad will be there. I reach for my anxiety meds and hope for the best. Surely, he won't waste his time to watch me squirm in his presence. Then again, he went to my hearing at the licensing board, where I didn't even need to be present. What is his angle? Making sure I'm punished? Before I head out the door, I say a silent prayer for protection and peace.

As I pull into the parking lot, I scan for his truck or a New Orleans Parish police car. I don't see either and hope he's not here. I feel like puking. I'm so nervous. I leave my phone in the car and make my way to the front doors of the Jefferson Parish courthouse. Thankfully, I see William waiting for me as soon as I step inside. After I walk through the metal detector, I reach him, and we shake hands as he escorts me to courtroom number two.

We take the front row seat, which resembles an old, wooden church pew. I hope I don't have to be here long.

William walks to the front and speaks to a young lady in a pantsuit. He makes his way to me after a whispered conversation with her.

"We should be first in front of the judge," he says quietly.

"Oh, really? They don't do alphabetical?"

"Nah, those that have attorneys appear first in front of the judge. Since we got here early enough, we should be first up on the docket."

"Oh, okay," I say, taking in my surroundings.

Fifteen minutes until court is set to begin and people are trickling in quietly taking seats. There's a gaggle of well-dressed attorneys vying for the attention of the young lady. She must represent the prosecution as a paralegal. Finally, the judge steps in, and we stand, welcoming his presence. He's an older gentleman pushing mid-50s with salt and pepper hair, a stern father-like figure, everything I imagine a judge would be.

The judge asks the young lady who they have first, and sure enough, she loudly calls, "Audrey Tribb!"

William nudges me to get up, and I follow his lead to the microphoned podium.

The judge says, "Please state your full name and address for the record."

"Audrey Tribb, 3592 Dauphine St, New Orleans, 70117."

The prosecution's paralegal then nodded to William.

William began, "William Stewart, representing council for Ms. Tribb. We are requesting the charges be dismissed on behalf of Ms. Tribb. Ms. Tribb and her company, Magnolia Maison, have settled with the client, Mr. Chad Ewing, and request the Jefferson Parish District Attorney to dismiss the charges."

A middle-aged man took the place of the paralegal and must be the Assistant District Attorney because he speaks next.

His nasal voice begins, "Judge, we are aware that Ms. Tribb and Mr. Ewing have settled their differences, and we are also moving to dismiss the charges against Ms. Tribb, pending she participates and completes the Pre-Trial Diversion Program."

My breath catches. I already know that that just means they're going to fine me. It's done! Internally I'm screaming. It's over, another one is gone. I can barely feel my feet underneath me as William and I head for the door. When the door quietly shuts, I can hear the muffled voice of the ADA calling the next person, and I can't help but grab William in a hug.

25

It's my dad's 60th birthday. I'm headed back to their house. It's gotten easier each time I go back there. However, I still can't look at their porch and not remember. I just don't linger for as long in my thoughts. Turning onto their street, their house comes into view, and I smile when I see the ferns are back out.

As I've slowly reintroduced myself to society, these gatherings have gotten easier. Sometimes we talk about what happened, other times we don't. They generally take my lead. Almost everyone knows now, and not one person has turned their back on me. Unwavering support that I didn't think possible. I'd support whoever was in this position. Why do I deserve any different?

"Hey, you!" My dad's face lights up, shaking me from my thoughts. He grabs me in a bear hug. He's always scratched my back when he sees me. I linger and let him, reminded of being a kid again. I hand him his birthday gift and walk inside to greet everyone else. Part of me feels normal but changed.

We're in the middle of eating when my phone rings. The sound doesn't cause anxiety anymore. That is until I see the name: Sonja. I quickly excuse myself and, without thinking, head for the porch.

"Hello?"

"Hi, Miss Audrey. How are you?" Her voice sounds chipper, and I relax.

"Hi there, I'm doing pretty well. How are you?" I say, still hesitant.

"Oh, I'm well, I'm well. I hadn't talked to you in a few months and just wondered how you were."

"That is incredibly thoughtful and kind of you." My heart is warmed knowing this didn't all end up bad.

We talk for a few minutes, and she nonchalantly brings up the topic of Ms. Broussard. I always forget that they live in the same tiny town.

"Have you heard about Ms. Broussard?"

"Uhh, no ma'am, is everything okay?"

"Oh yeah, everything is fine. Ms. Broussard has lost her home to foreclosure."

Nearly a year ago, I would've been pleased to hear this. I would've kept each of their heartaches like trophies on a shelf. Now, I have mixed feelings.

"My goodness, that's awful," I say honestly.

"Yes, it is. She's pretty devastated."

"Rightly so."

We sit in silence for a few seconds.

Sonja continues, "Not that I'd wish that on anyone, but you get back what you put out into the universe. You can't go around ruining people's lives and expect to live a worry-free life. I'm sorry to say so, but that's how life works."

"I wish I could say I disagree, but I think you're right."

"Is that why you didn't pursue these people, Audrey?" she asks sweetly.

"Yes, ma'am, that's exactly why. I couldn't be the cause of someone's heartache, it's just not in me."

"Well, God bless your sweet soul, young lady. Oh, I almost forgot, this was the main reason I was calling you. Remember that investigator with the Interior Design Board... oh what's her name?" She's talking so fast I can barely keep up.

My heart skips a beat, "Sandy Colefield?"

"That's it! Do you remember her?"

"Yes, ma'am, she was awful. She and Ms. Broussard took the lead on this whole thing."

"I know, sweetheart. Well, someone told me she was *fired*!"

"What?" I can't believe what I'm hearing. "Why?"

"No one knows, but I can guarantee it has to do with your case, Audrey," she seems excited to share this news with me.

"You think so?"

"Absolutely. I've only heard through the grapevine, and you know how reliable that can be, that she was put on leave in January, and then they let her go in March after they did some *investigation*." She emphasizes the last word as though she put air quotes around it.

"Wow." The chips continue to fall. Their decisions affected more than just me. When are people going to realize that for a moment, they may be in control, but God is on the throne?

"How's Jackie?" I ask, changing the subject to one Sonja will gladly switch to. I don't want to relish in someone else's misfortune, that's what they did to me.

We talk for another half hour. Everything would come back around; I just had to wait and watch. I don't feel like I thought I would, though. I feel sorry for them. Part of me wants to ask Ms. Broussard and Sandy Colefield if it was worth it. I guarantee they're too stubborn to realize and probably still blame me. Forever the victim. I refuse to be.

When we hang up, I sit on the porch a few minutes longer, watching the ferns sway in the breeze. Hanging there like nothing ever happened, lazily swinging in the sun.

They can twist and turn if they like, but they don't. They gently soak up the sun, unbothered. New fronds begin to unfurl, they're bigger this year. I'm amazed when I see they grew in winter when it was dark and cold. I stare in thought as I watch the ferns sunbathe. Everything to me is metaphorical these days. They were sheltered during the cold months, brought in for their protection. In many ways, I'm like these hanging ferns. Like me, the ferns were fine outside in their natural habitat. If they had thoughts, I'm sure they'd question why they were moved, taken out of what was familiar. What they didn't know was that winter was coming. Cold, dark days ahead. In many ways, I resemble them. God took me out of what could've wounded me and brought me inside. I'll never know what life would've looked like had I not been arrested. It very well could've been worse, but He scooped me up and temporarily hid me away where it was safer, where I could grow.

Once I get back inside, I tell my family all that Sonja told me. They count this as a victory, and they celebrate.

I make sure to go to church every Sunday morning, and I'm connecting with my church in ways I didn't imagine before. I've shared my testimony with my small group, which garnered lots of attention. People wanted to hear it, wanted to get to know me, and hear about how I was trying to change it. Make it better. Thankfully, I haven't signed any non-disclosure agreements, so technically, I can talk all I want to about it. Where I thought people would shun and shame me, they've come in droves to hear my story. Some ladies even approached me about joining a prison ministry. I said yes immediately. My pastor also encouraged me to start speaking at churches to share my testimony.

This Sunday was no different, as far as I knew. We listened to the sermon and waited for the altar call at the end of the service. My knees were nearly knocked from under me when I saw Chad heading to the altar. I thought there would never be a day that I didn't look into the driver's seat of a police car and expect to see Chad's face. Not here, not in my church. God, why would you do this to me?

"Go to him," a soft voice whispered in my head.

"God, please, no. Not now, I'm not ready for this."

"Go to him," the voice repeated.

My body wouldn't obey my mind, and I found myself walking up behind Chad, kneeling down with his back to me. I laid my hands on him and began to pray. I prayed for his heart and prayed for him to find peace. When the pastor was done praying, Chad stood up and turned around to see me. Months ago, I would've kept a painting above my fireplace of how his face looked at this moment—a mix of confusion, shock, and later guilt.

I chose not to speak. Instead, I gave him a smile, turned around, and went to my car, where I wept. My heart felt like it would explode out of my chest. I wanted to hold onto my anger. What did I have if I didn't have it? My anger was always bristling in the back as if it were on the back burner of my stove, waiting to boil over but not quite ready. Now, the burner was just turned off, my anger stolen from me. God freed me from it, not Chad. Ephesians 6:12 slams to the forefront of my mind: "For our struggle is not against flesh and blood, but against the rulers, against the authorities, against the powers of this dark world and against the spiritual forces of evil in the heavenly realms."

I wanted him to suffer. I didn't want to forgive, not now. The feeling that overwhelmed me that I thought was sorrow and anger turned out to be relief. I didn't realize how heavy the anger was that I was carrying around. My body longed to drop it, but my mind wasn't ready. I imagine Chad felt the same about me. Chad's heart of stone melted to one of flesh in that moment. It felt like an out-of-body experience watching the anger flee and the forgiveness takes its place. I had been walking around like the victim, and I needed to take ownership of my error. God worked on both Chad and me.

God brought me out of the cold, dark place that could have caused me so much more pain. Like the fern, I was just fine in my natural habitat. I had no reason to move or change anything. God plucked me out of my comfortable state, made me uncomfortable for a season to protect me, all to help me grow. And only now that it's over can I see how my fronds have unfurled and I'm growing. Growing is painful and confusing, but I needed to trust in the One who knew winter was coming.

About the Author

S. D. was born and raised in Louisiana, where the summers are sweltering and the seasons are Pollen, Mardi Gras, Crawfish, and College Football. She's left the state for short periods, finding her way to Texas and New Mexico, but she's always found herself coming back home. Although she did sneak the southwestern style back into the pelican state, who says Kokopellis and turquoise can't blend with Cajun motifs? Nah, we won't tell her either.

Book reviewing since 2016, she's been featured in San Francisco Book Review and Manhattan Book Review, as well as finding herself on the coveted reviewer lists of Penguin Random House and HarperCollins, to name a few. While she's always adored reading from a young age, S. D. loves the creative aspect of writing stories herself. What originally began as a gift to her father transformed into a much bigger story than she had planned. But as any good writer would do, she pivoted!

Her most passionate work is being a curriculum writer at the non-profit organization, The Hub in northern Louisiana. If you haven't checked out this incredible place, you're missing out!

S. D. lives in Louisiana with her husband, two children, and precious poodle, Mr. Darcy.